Blame it on the Mistletoe

Wedding wishes and Christmas kisses!

You're cordially invited to the wedding of Millie and Charlie. As long as some well-placed mistletoe and the temptation of festive flings don't get in the way...

When best friends Millie and Charlie decide to conveniently wed, they launch into the whirlwind of wedding planning. But when Charlie's called away on business, Millie's left with best man Giles as her stand-in groom. It's all going well until the sparks between them start to feel very real!

Meanwhile, Charlie has reconnected with his childhood friend Liberty. The gorgeous woman she's become knocks him off his feet, and soon he finds himself questioning his fake "I do" pact...

As Christmas Day approaches, will they go through with the wedding of the season? Find out in

Christmas Bride's Stand-In Groom
by Sophie Pembroke

Miss Right All Along
by Jessica Gilmore

Both available now!

Dear Reader,

I always love it when the opportunity arises for me to write linked books with other authors. In this case, writing a festive duet with the lovely Jessica Gilmore was pure joy! Christmas, weddings and romance... What more could anyone want from a book?

We had so much fun hashing out the shared backstory for our characters and pinpointing exactly where all their carefully laid plans for the future would be knocked off course by that most unexpected and unpredictable of things—true love.

Writing is often such a solitary job, and having someone to bounce ideas off of and debate character, conflict and Christmas with made this book such fun to write.

I hope you enjoy reading it every bit as much as I enjoyed writing it!

Love and mistletoe,

Sophie x

CHRISTMAS BRIDE'S STAND-IN GROOM

SOPHIE PEMBROKE

ROMANCE

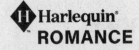

**Harlequin®
ROMANCE**

ISBN-13: 978-1-335-21617-5

Christmas Bride's Stand-In Groom

 Harlequin Enterprises ULC
22 Adelaide St. West, 41st Floor
Toronto, Ontario M5H 4E3, Canada
www.Harlequin.com

Printed in U.S.A.

Recycling programs for this product may not exist in your area.

Sophie Pembroke has been dreaming, reading and writing romance ever since she read her first Harlequin novel as part of her English literature degree at Lancaster University, so getting to write romantic fiction for a living really is a dream come true! Born in Abu Dhabi, Sophie grew up in Wales and now lives in a little Hertfordshire market town with her scientist husband, her incredibly imaginative and creative daughter, and her adventurous, adorable little boy. In Sophie's world, happy *is* forever after, everything stops for tea and there's always time for one more page...

Books by Sophie Pembroke

Harlequin Romance

Dream Destinations

Their Icelandic Marriage Reunion
Baby Surprise in Costa Rica

The Heirs of Wishcliffe

Vegas Wedding to Forever
Their Second Chance Miracle
Baby on the Rebel Heir's Doorstep

Twin Sister Swap

Cinderella in the Spotlight
Socialite's Nine-Month Secret

The Princess and the Rebel Billionaire
Best Man with Benefits

Visit the Author Profile page
at Harlequin.com for more titles.

To Jess, for saying yes to this duet!

Praise for
Sophie Pembroke

"An emotionally satisfying contemporary romance full of hope and heart, *Second Chance for the Single Mom* is the latest spellbinding tale from Sophie Pembroke's very gifted pen. A poignant and feel-good tale that touches the heart and lifts the spirits."

—*Goodreads*

CHAPTER ONE

MILLIE MYLES SAT back in her seat and laughed obligingly at the right moments in the best man's speech. Giles Fairfax was born to play the best man, really. He had the breeding, the training... Giles was polished, appropriate, wildly handsome in his morning suit, and his speech was going down well—the right proportion of laughs to groans and embarrassed blushes from the groom. Even she had laughed, against her will. He was *annoyingly* good at this.

Of course he'd always been annoyingly good at lots of things. Or sometimes just annoying. Even though they hadn't been in the same room since they were about eighteen—not an accident—Millie still had plenty of memories of Giles Fairfax before that, and stories from her best friend Charlie about his successes since, to hold against him.

Because Charlie was also *his* best friend. Giles and Millie had been competing for Number One Best Friend status since they were about twelve.

Childish? Yes. Was Millie still determined to win? Absolutely.

Before Giles came on the scene, it had been just her and Charlie. And since they'd become actual adults she'd managed to arrange things so that it still felt that way, most of the time—even if she knew Charlie and Giles got together often in her absence.

It had been something of a shock to see Giles Fairfax all grown up—no gangling eighteen-year-old youth any longer, but a broad-shouldered, confident and—damn it all—incredibly handsome thirty-year-old man. Before she'd realised who he was, she had to admit to even indulging in an appreciative look or two from behind.

Not that she'd ever do anything about it. Physical attraction was nothing compared to actual compatibility at a soul level. Millie had no interest in playing around with passion—she'd tried that before, and knew all too well where it led. She didn't want a guy who oozed charisma and charm—at least until he got bored with her in bed. No, next time she got involved with a man it would be a proper, grown-up relationship, based not on mutual desire, but on mutual beliefs and respect.

Was that really so much to ask?

Up at the top table, Giles still held the crowd in the palm of his hand. He told tales of mischievous university days at Oxford, which his audience all related to. Most of the guests had been to one or other of the elite English boarding schools beforehand, and after university gone on to work in the City, or the law, or medicine.

Millie was pretty sure she was the only state-educated florist in the bunch. She'd never felt more out of place in her life, and that was really saying something.

Up at the top table, Giles had paused for a laugh, smiling easily—until he looked over in her direction and, just for a second, caught her gaze. The smile fell away, and there was something else in his expression—something she couldn't quite read and didn't want to understand.

She looked down and focussed on the floral display in the centre of the table—one of those she'd spent all the night before reworking, because the bride had changed her mind about what she wanted—*again*—at the last moment.

She'd known Giles for more than half her life now, and even if they hadn't spent time together in over a decade her opinion of him hadn't changed in all those years. He was the quintessential posh boy, from a family with money, land and a title, gliding through life on other people's efforts and only ever putting on a show instead of being a real person.

It was that last part that made him different from the man she'd come to this wedding with. Their mutual best friend Charlie might have the land and the money, and the family title one day, but he knew what it was to work for it. When times—and renovation costs—had got tough, his family had turned their inherited good fortune into a thriving business that employed a lot of local people and small businesses. Giles's family, as far as she knew, had just pulled up their drawbridge and enjoyed their good fortune.

Her gaze moved to the bride, icily beautiful at the top table, and she squeezed her date's hand. Beside her, Charlie had a fixed smile on his face—a 'society smile' she called it. Because he sure as hell wasn't smiling inside. She knew that much.

The love of his life was marrying another man, and she'd never been as furious at anyone as she was at Octavia Sinclair right now. Even her almost two-decades-long annoyance with Giles faded into insignificance next to what Octavia had done to Charlie.

'You doing okay?' she murmured to Charlie, as Giles wound up the best man's speech with a heartfelt ending and received a round of applause that went on for a while.

'Of course,' Charlie said, clearly lying. 'Why wouldn't I be? I'm here with the most beautiful— and wonderful—woman in the room.'

The smile he gave her as he said the last bit was, at least, a real one, but Millie wondered if she should have cut him off from the champagne a little earlier.

'Seriously, Mills. Thank you for coming with me. Hanging out with you today has made it all a little bit more bearable.'

She leaned in and rested her head against his shoulder. 'I wouldn't be anywhere else.'

It wasn't strictly true. Attending a high society wedding with the sort of people Charlie had grown up with wasn't exactly her idea of a good time. But Charlie needed her. So of course she'd said yes when he'd asked her to attend the wedding. Even if Octavia's nose had wrinkled slightly when she realised that her ex-boyfriend was bringing her florist as his date.

It had meant that she could watch the fruits of her labours today, though. The glorious riot of autumnal colours she'd carefully arranged into an arch that the bride and groom had stood under for the ceremony. The trailing bouquet of honey and golden hues that the bride had discarded somewhere already. The turning leaves and blousy roses in the rustic-but-polished table decorations. It was nice to see her work being enjoyed. Octavia had wanted to wow everyone with the flowers, and Millie was pretty sure she'd pulled that off.

Usually she was gone before the guests arrived, so it made a nice change to see things through to the end.

Charlie reached for the champagne bottle again, and Millie began calculating how hard it would be to actually carry him out to the taxi at midnight. She was glad she'd decided to stick to just one small glass for the toasts. She needed her wits about her today. Besides, she needed to get used to cutting out alcohol.

There were black-tied waiters moving around the room with coffee pots, so she smiled hopefully at the nearest one and he made his way over, filling both their cups. Millie thanked him profusely—she was going to need the caffeine.

Something else you'll have to give up if you want to get pregnant.

The thought burst, uninvited, into her mind, and she dropped her teaspoon into her saucer with a clatter.

Charlie looked up, concerned. 'Okay?'

'Fine!' She beamed back at him. Today wasn't about her problems, it was about his. 'How are you doing?'

Charlie gave a small half-shrug, and an attempt at a smile. 'It is what it is.'

Oh, how she hated that phrase. The idea of lying down and accepting things. She wanted to *change* the stuff that made her miserable, or angry, or whatever.

She supposed there really wasn't very much Charlie could do about Octavia marrying another man, though. Or the fact that Octavia had been a stone-cold bitch since the first day Millie met her—not that Charlie had ever really seen that.

Millie was well aware that her perspective on the world—and especially on *Charlie's* rarefied and prosperous world—was from a different angle to his. She hadn't grown up in the splendour of Howard Hall, or at boarding school, attending society events with the same people with the same world view every season. Her parents didn't have a wardrobe of black-tie outfits ready for any occasion, or a cook on hand to cater and staff to serve when they hosted.

She'd grown up in the gatehouse at the hall, with a mother who *was* that cook and a father who'd cared for the gardens and grounds before he died. Charlie had been her first playmate, her childhood best friend since he was four and she was three, and even after he'd been shipped off to boarding school for most of the year. Even after he'd met Giles there, and she'd suddenly had to share best friend status with an aloof and difficult boy she didn't know.

The point was, Charlie knew her better than anyone, and she knew who he was behind the society smile.

But she'd never really been part of his world the way Giles had. That had given him an advantage in the Best Friend Battle.

She'd watched those Howard Hall parties and grand occasions from behind the bushes, seen

Charlie trotted out in a miniature suit to match his father's to make nice with his parents' friends and acquaintances. She'd stared with wide eyes as she took in what seemed to be a fairytale world— at least until one of her parents had found her and dragged her home to bed.

She shook the memories away. Here, now, she was an invited guest at the society wedding of the year, on the arm of one of the most eligible bachelors in the country—Charles St Clare Howard, heir to the title Baron Howard, which had links back to the Normans. None of the guests here knew that she was only attending for moral support in the role of childhood best friend. For all they knew she *belonged* here, and Charlie was wildly, madly in love with her. Maybe he was planning to propose. They could be thinking of starting a family—

Don't think about it, Mills.

Not today. Today wasn't a day for thinking about her problems—it was for distracting Charlie from his.

Which would be easier if the bride wasn't now bearing down on them in her designer wedding gown, feathers ruffling along the train and her icy beauty on full display.

'*There* you are,' she said, as if Millie hadn't been sitting in her assigned place on the seating plan for the last several hours. 'I need you to fix my bouquet.'

Millie got to her feet. 'What happened to it?'

Octavia shrugged delicate shoulders. 'No idea. But it looks uneven, and it needs to be *perfect* before I toss it later. Come on!'

Of course Octavia needed her flowers to look perfect before she threw and probably destroyed them for the cameras. Millie cast an apologetic look at Charlie, whom Octavia hadn't even acknowledged, and then followed her.

It was a reminder that, really, she was only staff. Just in case she'd been getting any ideas above her station.

Giles Fairfax had heard, often from ex-girlfriends, the phrase 'always the bridesmaid, never the bride'. But he'd never come across the idea of 'always the best man, never the groom'.

All the same, that seemed to be his lot in life. Octavia and Layton's wedding was the third time he'd been best man this year alone. Honestly, he was running out of material.

He suspected he was just a safe pair of hands. In the circles he ran in—or had done growing up, at least—everyone had a large group of friends, but close, best friends were less of a thing. And so, when prospective grooms started falling, one by one, they looked around for who was most likely to keep a wedding day calm, on track, and not humiliate them in his toast.

He did also have a bit of a reputation for organising some spectacular stag dos by now, so that might play into it, too.

It suited Giles well enough. It wasn't as if he had any intention of ever getting married himself anyway, but seeing so many other people's weddings up close and in all their bickering glory would have put him off if he did.

Not to mention what the grooms tended to get up to on the stag weekends.

He'd been conflicted about saying yes to this one, though. As much as he liked Layton, his opinion of Octavia was rather less positive. Not least because of the man she'd just left slumped at a table on the outer edges of the room, watching her sashay away in her wedding gown.

Or maybe he was watching the woman beside her...just a little bit. The dark-haired woman in the sage-green dress, helping the bride fix her bouquet. She had curves where Octavia had angles, was dark where the bride was icy blonde, and soft where she was sharp. If he didn't know the wicked tongue and disapproving stare she'd turn on him, Giles would be doing more than looking.

The moment he'd caught her gaze during his speech he'd felt the undeniable spark of attraction that usually boded very well for his evening. Except it was *Millie*, so it had confused more than excited him. And, of course, she'd looked instantly away. Clearly her opinion of him hadn't changed with the passage of time.

He hadn't seen Millie Myles in over a decade, but he had to admit he didn't remember that zing of chemistry between them when they were teenagers. More a zing of irritation and annoyance. But now... Now she was utterly gorgeous, and she walked with a confidence in herself she'd definitely never had at eighteen. He could absolutely understand Charlie asking her to this wedding as his date...except for the fact that until now Charlie had never given any indication that he saw Millie Myles as anything but his *other* childhood best friend.

Not that friendship was a competition, really. Except somehow it always had been for Giles and Millie. They'd battled over being the most important person in the world to Charlie—and somehow, in the process, let him fall into Octavia's clutches instead.

In all honesty, Giles was glad Charlie had Millie beside him today—especially since Giles himself had too many other duties to keep a close eye on him. Obviously he'd never admit as much to Millie herself, or even to Charlie. That wasn't how the dynamic between the three of them worked, and he could see no good reason to change it now.

Giles slipped into the now empty seat beside Charlie to check in on his friend, noting the empty bottle of champagne and full coffee cup in front of him.

'How's it going?'

It seemed an inadequate question. The real one was something more like, *Is your heart torn apart inside you, watching the woman you love marry another? How the hell are you still sitting upright? Why did you even agree to come?*

But they didn't ask those sorts of questions in his circles.

'Oh, Giles.' Charlie plastered on a smile that Giles didn't believe for a moment. 'It's been a lovely day. Great speech, by the way. You must be an old hand at this by now.'

'Just practising for when you ask me to be *your* best man.' Giles tilted his head towards where Millie was fussing with Octavia's bouquet, while the bride watched her like a hawk. 'Although since you brought *Millie* as your date to your ex's wedding, I guess that's still a way off?'

It occurred to Giles that if Charlie ever looked up and realised that Millie was a beautiful woman, and a thousand times better than Octavia, he'd probably promptly fall in love with her. And that would mean that Millie would *definitely* win the battle over Charlie they'd been engaged in since they were about twelve.

Maybe he should just let her. 'She did grow up well, though, I have to admit,' he said, staring over at Millie again. Probably it was just that long-lasting feud that made something inside him clench at the idea of Millie marrying Charlie.

'I notice *you* didn't bring a date, even though you're best man.' It was a clumsy attempt to change the subject on Charlie's part, but Giles went along with it.

'I never do—you know that.'

He had no intention of getting married— ever—and he was always worried about any of his casual hook-ups getting ideas if he brought them to something as meaningful as a wedding. There was just something about the atmosphere at these things.

Giles looked back over at Millie. At her gently curving body, the dark hair falling over her shoulders, the slightly irritated look on her face as Octavia bossed her around. Was *she* getting ideas? Did she want more than friendship from Charlie after all these years?

He wouldn't put it past her. And if Millie finally wanted to change their relationship, it might just wake Charlie up from his Octavia obsession.

If that happened… Well. Giles would just have to work very hard at being happy for his best friend.

And start working on his next best man's speech.

He decided to test his theory.

'So, if you two are just friends, as always, and I don't have a date—'

'No.' Charlie interrupted him before he could even get the thought out.

Yeah, they're still just friends. Not buying it.

'Why not?' Giles raised his eyebrows in innocent query. 'It's not like we're strangers hooking up at a wedding. We've known each other for ever, and we're not the same bickering teenagers we were back then. Although maybe we were just trying to hide a deeper attraction...'

'Because...she's not your type,' Charlie tried.

Looking at the way Millie had grown into her curves, and her confidence, Giles had to disagree.

'Oh, I think she looks *exactly* my type.'

Gorgeous and confident and curvy and *luscious.* He'd only said it to needle Charlie into admitting his feelings—but that didn't mean it wasn't true. If they'd met now, for the first time, Giles knew he would have been interested in getting to know Millie better. For a night, at least. But God, what a night... If she channelled all that passion she'd managed to bring to their teenage fights into his bed, it would be *explosively* good.

Hell. He *really* wanted Millie Myles. That was new.

'Absolutely not.' Charlie's voice was, if anything, even firmer this time. 'Millie is...she's my oldest friend.'

'Because I'm your *best* friend,' Giles put in, automatically. It was a reflex born of years of feeling he was competing with Millie for that title, he supposed.

'And I know that she is looking for commitment—for a real happy-ever-after and true love and a family—everything you go out of your way to avoid,' Charlie finished. 'So, no. She is not your type.'

Giles shuddered at the very idea. Time to let the fantasy go.

Yes, one night with Millie Myles would be something spectacular, he was sure. But he didn't mess around with women looking to settle down.

'Fair enough, then.' He looked between Charlie and Millie again and smiled. Well, if he couldn't have her... 'If only there was someone else here who wants the same things she does...'

Charlie took his meaning at last and rolled his eyes. 'Go away, now. She's coming back, and I don't want you to get tempted and abandon reason.'

Giles laughed and stood up, nodding politely at Millie and Octavia as he headed for the bar, and trying not to notice how attractive the confused little frown line between Millie's eyebrows was.

Charlie was right—she really wasn't his type. Which was a shame. But maybe he'd be best man again sooner than he thought, if he was reading the signs right.

CHAPTER TWO

CHARLIE WAS GROWING more and more morose as the evening wore on. Millie had given up trying to ration the champagne, and instead settled for trying to distract him. She scanned the dance floor for something, or someone, to talk about— but got immediately distracted by the sight of Giles Fairfax dancing with one of the bridesmaids.

Damn him. Couldn't he even be bad at dancing?

It wouldn't bother her so much, except that every time she glanced his way she got that funny feeling in the pit of her stomach—the sort she'd used to get when her junior school crush walked past her desk. Which was ridiculous, given that she was a grown woman now, and certainly not interested in Giles Fairfax in a childish crush way or any other.

It didn't help that he caught her looking every single time, either.

She glanced away, but not before Giles had

caught her gaze and smiled, low and warm, then whispered something in his dance partner's ear. Probably mocking her. That would be about right.

Charlie reached for his glass again, and she got back to the task in hand. Distraction. Which, at a wedding, meant gossip.

'Those two definitely had an argument before the wedding.' Millie nodded towards the couple dancing past them. 'They were glaring at each other in the church.'

'Were they?' Charlie sounded surprised. 'I didn't notice.'

'Because you were staring at the bride.'

'True.'

Charlie leaned against her, as they both gazed around the room.

'I think she was hoping he'd propose before now,' he said, after a moment. 'They've been dating long enough.'

'How long is "long enough"?' Millie asked absently.

She'd dated her ex, Tom, for three years and they'd never got close. She'd assumed they were just too young, until the day she'd found him in bed with his work colleague. Apparently the passion had faded between them and he needed to get his kicks elsewhere.

Obviously she knew, intellectually, she was better off without him—and that she'd learned an important lesson from his betrayal: not to trust good sex and mutual attraction to turn into a lasting relationship. But it was still depressing to realise now that he might have been her best chance at the future she wanted.

God help me if that's *the case.*

Charlie shrugged. 'I don't know. Octavia and I were together for years—'

'Except you broke up every six months or so,' Millie pointed out.

'That might have been the problem.' His glass still hung precariously from his fingers, but he never spilled a drop.

'Not the only problem,' Millie said. 'She was also awful to you, and the whole relationship was toxic, and I wanted better for you because I love you and you're one of my very favourite people.'

'And you're one of mine.'

He gave her a sloppy hug, and she felt tears prick her eyes. She really should have said no to that last glass of wine.

'You know, I don't think I'll ever get married now,' Charlie went on, still staring morosely over at where Octavia was dancing with a group of her bridesmaids—minus the one who was still snuggled up against Giles's shoulder. Not that she was watching them. 'I think Octavia was my one shot. If I couldn't make it work with her...' He shook his head. 'Except I have to, somehow. There's the estate. The title. The entail. My family expect—no, they *need* me to marry and carry on the line. But how can I? She was my one true love. How can I marry someone else?'

'I don't believe that.' Millie stopped watching Giles and reached over to take Charlie's hands in hers. 'I know it hurts now, but…you have to have faith. I thought that Tom was my one shot—'

'And you haven't dated anyone seriously since. Remind me how this is supposed to convince me?'

Millie sighed. The man had a point.

'I guess *I* just have to have faith,' she said. 'I saw the doctor the other day and—'

'Is everything okay?' Suddenly Charlie's full attention was on her, his eyes wide with concern. 'What did they say.'

'Nothing like that,' she assured him. 'But I'd been having some tests for…well, women's stuff. And it turns out that my fertility is declining a lot faster than is usual for someone in their late twenties. They reckon that if I want to start a family I need to either freeze my eggs and hope, or get started now.'

Charlie let out a long breath. 'I'm sorry. I know how much having a family means to you.'

Her whole life it had only been her, her mum and her dad. No extended family, no cousins or siblings. Then her dad had died when she was fifteen, and it had become just her and mum. One day, it would just be her.

Millie had always imagined a large family…

grandkids for her mum to spoil, a loving husband there to share the load. Now…it seemed that dream might already be over before it had started.

'What are you going to do?' Charlie asked.

'Find someone to fall madly in love with me in the next forty-eight hours and marry them after a whirlwind courtship, settle down and have kids as soon as possible, and live happily ever after?'

It was a joke. Of course it was a joke.

It was just also what she wanted most in the world.

Charlie was still looking at her. She sighed.

'I guess I'll look into getting my remaining eggs frozen. Hope that things work out later.' She shrugged. 'Not many other options, are there?'

Charlie looked thoughtful. 'Maybe *we* should just get married. Could solve a lot of problems.'

Millie laughed. 'Can you imagine? My mum would be over the moon.'

'So would mine.' The music changed to something faster, more upbeat, and he held out a hand to her. 'Come on. If we have to do this wedding, let's at least do it properly and get a good boogie in.'

The best man dancing with the bride was probably one of those things that was on a checklist of 'must-haves for the perfect wedding day' somewhere—certainly Giles had been roped into it at all the other weddings he'd attended recently.

Sometimes the bride in question used the dance to berate him for the hungover state of the groom at the church, other times to thank him for keeping the stag do under control.

Octavia, however, didn't seem interested in talking to him at all while they moved to the music. Stiff in his arms, she stared over his shoulder, so Giles tried to manoeuvre them so he could figure out what she was looking at.

Oh, of course. Charlie was dancing with Millie just behind them.

Giles had never tried to understand what kept Octavia and Charlie together—and then apart and then together again—over the years. He'd just figured that love was unfathomable. They weren't good for each other, though—that was clear to anyone with eyes.

And if Charlie and *Millie* really could find happiness together, maybe he should start rooting for them. Instead of imagining a different world in which *he* was the one taking Millie home tonight.

It really was a peculiar change of pace to find himself wanting to spend time with her, rather than avoid her completely.

'They make a nice couple, don't you think?' He only said it to needle Octavia, and was rewarded by a scowl.

'I just can't believe he brought my *florist* to the wedding as his date!' she snapped back.

'You know full well that they're very old friends.'

Octavia rolled her eyes. 'Yes, well… Sometimes the friends we make in our youth aren't supposed to follow us through to adulthood.'

Despite her words, Octavia had managed to manoeuvre them closer to the other couple and, before Giles realised what she was doing, the bride slipped out of his arms and cut in between Charlie and Millie, saying, 'Bride's prerogative.'

Which left Giles and Millie standing staring at each other. Alone. In the past, Giles had gone out of his way to avoid moments like this. But today was a rather different sort of day, and he was discovering all sorts of new emotions about Millie Myles, so after a second, he offered her his arm. 'May *I* have this dance?'

She shrugged, looking as surprised as he felt. 'Sure.'

He wondered if she sensed it, too—the way things had changed between them. Maybe it was just meeting again as adults, as whole people who had more in their lives than a feud over who could be a better friend to Charlie. A chance to see each other in a new light.

Whatever it was, Giles had to admit it had him off balance.

Being attracted to a woman wasn't exactly new ground for him—usually he'd take them home or he wouldn't, but either way he wouldn't think about them again. Wanting a woman he couldn't have wasn't familiar, but still not outside the realm of his experience.

Finding himself so passionately wanting a woman he'd always hated was definitely new, though.

The band had changed tempo again, to a slow, crowd-pleasing old standard. Giles wondered if Octavia had personally approved the set list and had known this was coming up next. He wouldn't put it past her.

'She still can't quite take her claws out of him, can she?' Millie said softly, unknowingly echoing his own thoughts as they watched Charlie dance with the bride.

'She's always wanted to have her cake and eat it,' Giles said. 'Actually, I think she wants the whole bakery.'

Millie gave him a small flash of a smile. That was definitely new, too. Before, she'd always scowled at him.

'You don't sound very approving. And yet you agreed to be her husband's best man. What were you thinking, Giles?'

He shifted his arms slightly, bringing her in a little closer. It was easier to dance that way, that was all. Nothing to do with the way she felt against his body. Warm and soft and… She'd asked a question, hadn't she?

'Oh, I'm basically a best man for hire these

days,' Giles admitted. 'A safe pair of hands. I won't let the groom get *too* wasted before the wedding, but I'll make sure he has enough fun that he doesn't feel he missed out. I give a good speech, and mothers-in-law love me. This is my third wedding this year.'

'I should have known that wearing a suit and tie and being charming would end up being your ultimate skill set.'

She laughed, and he felt it reverberate inside his chest. She was taking him over, and he couldn't help but imagine how much closer they *could* be.

'You know me,' he said, making it sound easy and careless, even though it felt anything but. And even though it wasn't true. She *didn't* know him. He'd made sure she—and the rest of the world—never did. Except for Charlie. Charlie was an exception—for both of them, he suspected.

Another reason he had to stop noticing the way her breasts brushed against his shirt. She wasn't for him. And she could never know the truth.

Giles played the part, the game, and smiled and charmed, but he never let on that underneath it all he was fighting tooth and nail. Nobody saw his struggles—with his family, his finances, his own sense of fairness—because he didn't put them on show, and nobody looked too deep. They knew his name, his family, and that was all they needed to know to make their assumptions about who he was.

He wasn't about to let Millie Myles know any different. But she was distracting him with her closeness. With the chemistry between them that had taken him by such surprise.

Maybe it was because she *didn't* play the game. She probably didn't even know what the game was.

If he'd never met her before today Giles would have known that Millie didn't belong to the same sort of society that he—and almost every other guest in the room—had grown up in. Not because she didn't look the part, or because she'd done anything particular to give it away. But because of that laugh.

It was too honest, too real, to belong in his world.

His world was filled with fake smiles and polite amusement. With saying one thing, then turning around and saying the opposite to the next person. Everyone played the game, played the room, and said or heard what would get them where they wanted to be. They traded favours, not jokes.

But Millie laughed as if she found him funny, rather than because she was buttering him up for something. It was strangely refreshing. And probably the result of the excellent champagne Octavia was serving, because she'd definitely never found him funny before.

'You should set up a website offering your best man services,' she said. 'I'd recommend you to my brides.'

'Octavia said you were responsible for the incredible wedding flowers. I knew you were a florist, but this…it's really great, Millie.' He could give her a compliment. That wasn't *flirting*, exactly. Just a sign that they were adults now, not bickering teens.

Millie snorted. Something else none of the young ladies he'd grown up with would ever do in company. Well, not his company, anyway.

'You mean she told you she couldn't believe Charlie brought the florist to her wedding as his date.'

'You heard her?' Normally Octavia was more discreet with her catty comments, but maybe a florist didn't deserve discretion in her eyes.

'Just a guess.'

She glanced over to where they'd last seen Charlie and Octavia, but either they'd got swept away to the other side of the dance floor, or Charlie had made a rapid escape from the clutches of his ex. Either way, apparently Giles's fate was always to be dancing with someone who was looking for someone else.

All things considered, that was probably for the

best. Weddings gave people ideas, and God forbid he—the eternal bachelor—start getting any.

He'd seen what wedded bliss did to people, especially in his family, and he had no desire to propagate that misery down to another generation, thank you.

'I'm hoping that Charlie will be asking for my services next, now he's clearly over Octavia,' he said, raising an eyebrow at her suggestively.

'Charlie? Oh, we're not… I'm not here as his *date*, Giles. Well, I am. But not *that* sort of date. You know it's not like that between us.'

'I know… I know. You've always been just friends,' Giles said, to stop her rambling. 'I just thought… I know you and I haven't always got along, but honestly…? It's so nice to see him with someone who actually *likes* him, for a change. He deserves to be happy. And aren't all the best relationships ones that are founded in friendship? Come on, Millie. You can't tell me you've never even *thought* about it.'

Just because *Giles* had no intention of marriage, he still wanted that happiness for his friends. And Charlie, he knew, *wanted* all the things that Giles hoped to cast aside. The wife, the kids, the family, the estate and the title carrying on in perpetuity.

And if Charlie got together with Millie, maybe Giles could stop thinking about her this way.

She'd be firmly off limits then, and Giles would never, ever mess with his best friend's girl.

'He *does* deserve that,' Millie said quietly. Then she looked up at him with a sad smile. 'My mum always says that marrying her best friend was the best decision she ever made. She still says it now, even though Dad's been gone for years.'

'I'm sorry.'

Giles could tell from the sudden glassiness of her eyes that the loss still hurt. He remembered the day he'd died; Giles had been visiting Charlie for the summer, like he often did, and he'd made one of his usual digs at Millie…and Charlie had yelled at him. The only time he'd ever done it. Giles had run and hid in the orchard, and it had been hours later that Charlie came and explained what was going on.

Now, Millie just shrugged, which made her lose time with the music, and Giles tightened his arm around her waist to get them back on track. It pressed her even closer against him, and he swallowed as he tried to ignore the sensation.

Get it together, Fairfax. She's talking about her dead father, for God's sake.

'It's been a long time,' Millie said. 'But Charlie has been a good friend to me—and to you. His whole family have. I knew today would be hard for him, and I wanted to be here to support him. Even if it is wildly obvious to everyone else that I don't really belong here.'

'I wouldn't say "wildly obvious"…'

Except it was. Not because of Millie, exactly. Just because everyone else in this room knew each other—had been coming to events like this, where the guest list was almost exactly the same, for ever. There were a few other outliers—not to mention the American contingent—but he'd heard a few people asking who the woman on Charles Howard's arm was.

'Just not as obvious as Layton's crowd.'

She laughed. 'That's true. Maybe I should affect an American accent. *Whaddaya reckon?*' she asked, in the most outrageous Southern drawl he'd ever heard, surprising a laugh from him.

'Perfect,' he said. Then he sobered. 'You know, it really was good of you to come for Charlie today.' He knew she must feel uncomfortable attending as a guest, rather than a supplier—and Octavia clearly hadn't done anything to ease that feeling. But she'd come anyway. 'I'm glad he has you in his corner. Especially since I had other duties.'

The music came to a close and she stepped out of his arms. 'So am I. And now I'd better go and track him down. Thanks for the dance.'

She turned and walked away, her sage-green dress swishing around her legs as her hips swayed, and Giles found he couldn't help but watch her go.

Somehow, the room felt a little colder without her in his arms.

Swallowing hard, he shook the feeling away, and turned to find out when the bride and groom intended to cut the cake. He had best man duties to attend to.

The invitation Charlie had shown her had said 'carriages at midnight', and so, as the clock struck twelve, right on cue a fleet of taxis arrived outside Octavia's ancestral home to ferry the guests away again.

Charlie had sunk at least a couple of drinks at the bar since their dance, and Millie had to admit to another glass of wine or three, too, so they wrapped their arms around each other as they made their way down the stone steps at the front of the manor towards a cab.

Thankfully, Charlie's own sprawling family home, Howard Hall, wasn't far away—Charlie and Octavia's families were actually neighbours, although the size of the estates meant it still wasn't a safely walkable distance home at this time of night.

Or after quite so much to drink.

She glanced back over her shoulder as they waited for their cab driver to pull up and open the door. On the steps she saw Giles, watching them. He raised a half-full champagne flute in her direction and smiled.

Millie looked away. Today had been complicated and difficult enough without throwing

Giles Fairfax into the mix. She definitely wasn't going to spend any time thinking about how surprisingly lovely it had felt to have Giles's arms around her as they danced, or that it might have been the first time in history when they'd actually managed to talk and joke without sniping at each other. Much.

And she *definitely* wasn't dwelling on that feeling in the pit of her stomach. Or the sparks she felt between them every time their gazes met.

'Come on,' she told Charlie as she helped him into the car. 'Time to go.'

Today had just been far too weird for her to handle any longer. She and Giles had even *agreed* about something—even if that something was Charlie.

'Are you going to come home with me tonight?' Charlie asked into her shoulder, as the cab bumped its way along the endless driveway. 'Or wake up your mum?'

That was a no-brainer. 'I'll stay with you.'

It was what they'd done all through their late teens and early twenties, whenever they were both home and fancied a night out. Inevitably Millie would end up staying with Charlie rather than waking up her mum by stumbling into the tiny gatehouse cottage in the early hours of the morning.

It all felt so familiar—setting up the daybed in the living room area of Charlie's suite, pouring pint glasses of water and finding paracetamol for the morning, then curling up together under all the blankets and cushions to debrief the night. They might have been home from university for the Christmas holidays, still twenty and clueless.

Howard Hall still belonged to Charlie's family, free and clear, but large portions of it—the most showy, oversized areas—were mostly just used for events these days. The family had claimed the East Wing for their own, however, and modernised and done it up tastefully. Charlie's suite there was still four times the size of her own flat above Holly and Ivy, the florist shop that she ran, and that was before she even took the communal spaces in the wing into account. There were spare rooms, too, but she'd always preferred to stay with Charlie than use them.

Now, she curled up on the daybed, wrapped in a cashmere throw and leaning against cushions that had probably cost more than her actual bed at home, watching Charlie pour them one last nightcap.

'I think that went about as well as it could be expected to, don't you?' he said, weaving slightly as he crossed the room towards her.

She took her drink and held it to one side as he dropped, heaving himself onto the mattress next to her.

'I give them six months,' she said loyally. 'A year, tops.'

'You're probably right.' Charlie took a long sip of his drink. 'What do you think it is? The secret to an actual happy relationship, I mean.'

Ah, so they'd reached the philosophical portion of the evening. 'Well, my mum always said the secret was marrying your best friend,' she said, remembering the conversation she'd had with Giles while they danced.

He'd been a good dancer. And he seemed to really care about Charlie.

That was probably the only reason she was still thinking about him. Still imagining his arms around her.

'Going by that rule, I should probably marry you.' Charlie looked up at her with bleary eyes, smiling as he spoke.

Millie laughed, because of course he was joking.

Except…

'Giles thinks we should get married, too,' she said.

Was that proof that, whatever sparks she'd felt between them, he had felt nothing? Why else would he have suggested she and Charlie could be a match? Oh, God, he'd probably guessed that she was having some highly inappropriate and never-to-be-repeated crush-like feelings about him and been trying to let her down gently.

And she'd thought she'd got through the wedding without experiencing utter humiliation.

Looked like she'd relaxed too soon on that front…
Who knew what else she'd realise or remember
when she sobered up fully?

'Did he, now? Interesting.'

Something about Charlie's voice made her sus-
picious. He never could hide anything when he
was drunk. And if Giles had said anything to him
about her, she needed to know now. For damage
control purposes.

'Interesting how?'

'Just that he said something similar to me,'
Charlie replied. 'I was warning him off you at
the time.'

That burned more than she'd thought it would.
It wasn't like she'd planned on *doing* anything
about her crush, but it still hurt to know that
Charlie disapproved. And she could guess exactly why.

'Because I'm not good enough?'

'Because you're far *too* good.' Charlie grabbed
her hand—the one not holding her drink—and
squeezed it tight. 'You're one of the best people
I know, and you deserve everything you want in
this world. And you want a family, and a happy-
ever-after—and we both know that is the last
thing that Giles wants.'

Of course it was. Even if this stupid feeling
in her stomach outlasted the hangover she was
bound to have tomorrow, it didn't matter. She'd
never do anything about it for plenty of reasons.

Starting with how attraction didn't lead to lasting relationships, and that was what she needed if she wanted to start a family. Then there was the fact that compatibility of goals and dreams mattered far more to her than passion. And Giles, as Charlie pointed out, didn't want the things she did.

'But *you* do,' Millie said.

His words had taken that burning feeling of not being enough and turned it into the sort of warmth that filled her chest and made her feel loved. And with that warmth came a realisation. One that she felt in the moment could change her whole life.

'You want the same things I do—to get married, be happy, have a family to carry on your name and title.'

Her gaze met his before he leaned back, just a fraction, and for a moment something hung in the air between them.

Something with potential.

It wasn't romance, or the sort of love that poets wrote about. It wasn't even close to the frisson she'd felt when she'd looked into Giles's eyes as they danced, or the way her blood had hummed as she'd been pressed against him.

It wasn't passion. But that was good. Passion never lasted.

Instead, it was something that made her feel safe and cherished.

And that was more important than passion. Wasn't it?

'*We* should get married.'

Millie honestly couldn't say for sure which one of them spoke the words first. The idea was just there, fully formed, in the room with them, and neither of them could ignore it.

She could marry her best friend, have the family she longed for, despite her failing fertility, and she'd never have to worry about anything like bad first dates or walking home alone at night again.

Millie had never thought she was the sort of woman who wanted to be looked after—she'd certainly never considered marrying for money or status. But marrying a man she loved, even if not romantically, so that they could take care of *each other*...

Now, that was the kind of plan she could get behind.

Of course, she was also kind of drunk. And so was he. She could never hold him to anything he agreed to after a day like today. And there was a chance this was utterly insane. She'd never, ever thought about Charlie that way. But then, she'd never thought about Giles and imagined him kissing her until today, either.

Oh, boy, she was definitely drunk if she was admitting that—even in her head.

Charlie opened his mouth to speak again, and she pressed a finger to his lips. 'Let's... We need to sleep on this. Sober up. Think things through. We'll talk about it in the morning.'

'And if we still think it's a good idea in the cold light of day?' Charlie asked.

'Then we'll start wedding planning.'

CHAPTER THREE

GILES'S PHONE RANG just as he was ushering the last—and most drunken—of the wedding guests into the remaining taxis. He ignored it.

Up ahead, he saw Charlie and Millie climbing into a cab, arms around each other and both giggling. Something inside his chest ached at the sight, and his brain helpfully reminded him how good she had felt in his arms.

If she was a different woman, or he was a different man, maybe things would be going differently this night. But they weren't, and they wouldn't. However tempting the idea might be.

He shook the thought away. Far better for her to be with Charlie tonight. And at least it seemed that they had enjoyed the day. Octavia, meanwhile, was stamping her feet somewhere behind him, but he was choosing to ignore it.

For a minute or two Giles enjoyed the stillness of the night, watching the last of the revellers leave.

Then his phone rang again.

Reaching into his pocket, he saw that he already had three missed calls, all from the same unknown number. The one that was calling now.

Well, that boded well...

He swiped to answer. 'Giles Fairfax.'

'Gilly! Oh, good, I've caught you.'

Only one person called him Gilly—and got away with it. Barely. And only one person would sound so upbeat about calling him repeatedly at gone midnight.

'Rebekah. What's happened? What do you need?'

His sister only ever called him if there was a problem, after all.

'Oh, just a tiny thing. I seem to be locked out of the house again. Do you think you could bring your spare set of keys over and let me in?'

Her tone was too light, too artificially inconsequential for him to believe that was all it was.

Besides, this had happened before.

'Where's Marc? Where are the kids, for that matter?'

He already knew the answer. But he was damned if he was going to go over there again without her saying it.

'Oh, they're inside. But they're asleep. It's late, you know. I don't want to wake them.'

But you'll wake me.

Not that he'd been asleep this time, but he

knew from past experience that it wouldn't have mattered if he had been.

'I'm on my way.' He hung up.

Lucky for Rebekah that he'd only had the one glass of champagne to toast with at this wedding and made it last all night. Plus his car was parked in the garage around the back. He hadn't even taken his overnight bag into the room assigned to him here, after spending last night at a local hotel with the groom.

He grabbed his tailcoat and keys and headed for the garage.

His already sour mood—it was never fun being the only sober person at a wedding—sank further. What was he doing, standing up beside Layton and all his other friends, watching them sign themselves up for a life of misery or causing one for someone else? He'd thought he could believe in the magic of love for others, even if not for himself, but with every wedding that passed it became harder.

His parents hadn't exactly started him off with the best example, he supposed. Despite loathing each other openly for his entire childhood, still neither one of them would leave and risk losing the lifestyle they'd grown accustomed to. The same way they wouldn't leave the ancient pile of Fairfax Lodge, even as it fell apart around their ears.

They liked the trappings of aristocracy—the

house, the title, the invitations, the society. But they'd do nothing to keep up their entitlement to it. Charlie's family, realising times and fortunes had changed, had leveraged their land, turned their property into a flourishing events business—not just providing lots of local employment but also using at least some of their staggering profits to benefit the people and the area around them.

Giles's parents would do nothing of the sort. They wanted the life they'd been born into without making any acknowledgment that the world they'd started in no longer really existed.

The home that Rebekah shared with her husband—a large, Georgian house in an acre or two of land—was thankfully no more than a forty-minute drive from Octavia's family estate. Giles's car crunched up the gravel drive, its headlights flashing off the bricks and the gardens, before landing on his sister, sitting shivering on the doorstep. With a sigh, Giles killed the engine and stepped out of the car.

'What was it this time?' he asked as he approached, his keys in hand.

'I must have just left them in another bag,' Rebekah said, unconvincingly. 'And you know how the kids need their sleep.'

Giles kept hold of the keys even as she tried to take them. 'Bekah. It's late. I've had a long day and driven all the way over here. So don't mess me about. What was it this time?'

'He didn't want me to go out.' Her shoulders slumped as she spoke. 'He doesn't approve of the other mothers at the village school, but Benjy isn't old enough for boarding school yet, whatever he says, so I *have* to see them. And I didn't want to offend them by not going tonight, or Benjy will be ostracised, won't he?'

She looked up at him with wide eyes, looking for absolution, but it wasn't his to give. More than that, she shouldn't need it.

'He took your keys again?'

She nodded. 'And you know how he'll be if I wake him up. So I called you.'

Giles nodded. 'Right.'

Anger coiled in his stomach. This wasn't the first time he'd been called out to let his sister into her own home because his brother-in-law had taken her keys in protest at her going out.

She'd never call him if there was another way out—he knew that much.

'How do you think he'll react if *I* wake him up?'

Rebekah's eyes widened even further. 'Gilly, no! We've talked about this. You might not approve of my marriage, but it's not your business, or your place to judge me for it.'

'I'm not judging you. I'm judging him.'

And he did. Regularly. Rebekah seemed to have

echoed their parents' marriage, more or less directly, and she still chose to live it out every day.

'Well, don't,' she snapped. 'This is my choice. I chose him, and this house, and this life and my family. And I'm not going to give it up just because he was in a bad mood about me going out tonight.'

She grabbed the keys from his hand and opened the door, before handing them back again.

'Thank you for coming out here,' she said, as she slipped inside. 'Goodnight, Giles.'

And there he was, left on his sister's doorstep in the middle of the night, feeling frustrated and impotent and hating marriage more than ever.

If he ever believed that his brother-in-law's behaviour had gone further—if he hurt her or the kids, or cut Rebekah off from her friends and family, or controlled her finances—he'd have grounds to step in. If she ever asked him to get her out, he'd do it in a heartbeat.

But instead she seemed content to defy her husband, then call Giles to let her into her own home. To argue, loudly, when she and Marc were alone—but put on a happy face in front of the children and company.

She chose to stay. For the same reasons, he assumed, that his parents clung on to a life long gone. For appearances. For the lifestyle they all wanted.

No wonder he'd decided to swear off both love

and marriage early on. Theirs was a legacy he wanted to cut short here and now.

From nowhere, a memory of Charlie and Millie with their arms around each other, laughing, came to his mind. Millie's words quickly followed.

'My mum always says that marrying her best friend was the best decision she ever made.'

Maybe if he'd ever had a friend like that—one who loved him through everything…who supported him as he supported them…one he could love—maybe then he'd feel differently.

But he didn't. He wouldn't even know where to start.

Charlie and Millie had fallen into each other's lives and hearts effortlessly. He'd always been an extra, a spare part, getting in their way, not quite sure how to find his own place. Always battling to matter to Charlie against the unbreakable bond he had with the girl next door. And he'd certainly never found his own Millie.

Love, it seemed, had never been an issue in his family. Love was not required, only an appropriate partner. Love wasn't something his family had taught him anything about.

Giles had had enough of the whole damn lot of them.

But, since Octavia's estate would be locked up by now, his London flat was too far to drive to at this time of night, and Rebekah clearly had no intention of antagonising her husband further by inviting him to stay, it seemed he'd have to deal with at least two more family members before he left again for the city.

Easing back into the car, he turned over the engine and headed for his parents' crumbling ancestral pile.

Millie's head throbbed and her tongue seemed to have doubled in size. But somewhere she could smell coffee brewing. And…and was that bacon? Bacon could fix a lot of ills, in her experience.

She experimented with opening her eyes and, having successfully achieved that, sat up and took a long gulp of the water in the pint glass beside her daybed.

The previous evening's activities and conversations trickled back into her consciousness.

Octavia being ridiculous about her bouquet and stealing Charlie for a dance.

Dancing with Giles. God, practically *lusting* after Giles Fairfax, of all possible people. She hoped he hadn't noticed. She'd never live that humiliation down. Giles had already witnessed one humiliation of hers in the past, and she wasn't keen to add to it.

What else? Drinking some more with Charlie, and coming back to his place to sleep it off, and…

What had happened then? She felt sure there was something more.

The room swam into focus and she blinked in the direction of the kitchen area of the suite. Charlie stood barefoot at the stove, frying bacon, the coffee machine whirring beside him. She shuffled out of bed, glad she always left a pair of pyjamas in his bottom drawer for nights such as last night. She'd made it halfway across the room before a memory from the previous evening hit her. Hard.

'Did we agree to get married last night?'

Charlie turned slowly to face her, his own face tired and a little grey. At least she wasn't the only one suffering.

'That is entirely possible, yes,' he replied. 'Coffee?'

'God, yes, please. In a bucket, if possible.'

The coffee was served, of course, in perfectly matching china mugs. Charlie sat opposite her at the small kitchen table and they stared at each other.

It felt as if they were each waiting for the other to laugh and say how ridiculous the idea was. And part of Millie wanted to do exactly that.

I mean, how did I get from dancing with Giles Fairfax to agreeing to marry Charlie?

Except…

Was it so ridiculous? Really?

She loved Charlie. She trusted Charlie. He made her laugh, and she was pretty sure they could make each other happy. That was more than a lot of people went into a marriage with, wasn't it?

For a moment, another flash of memory lit up her brain. A memory of dancing with Giles the night before, and how she'd felt as if her body knew his—knew how it would move against hers. The spark of… Attraction wasn't a strong enough word. The *want* that had flooded her from just being close to him had been something she wasn't sure she'd ever experienced before. Let alone with someone she'd basically disliked for the better part of twenty years.

But that was just lust—and probably champagne. Sexual attraction was easy—she'd had plenty of that with Tom at the start, and look how that had ended up. The passion had faded, and they'd slowly realised they had nothing else in common—but not before *he'd* realised he could have that passion with other women he hooked up with through dating apps.

She'd thought he would be her for ever person, even though he'd never talked about marriage. Now she knew she'd had a lucky escape. But it still hurt that she'd wasted so much time on someone who could treat her that way, who rated lust above love. Especially now that she knew her ovaries didn't have that kind of time to waste.

No, passion *definitely* wasn't a sign of anything.

But friendship was.

'We'd need to have rules,' she said, before she could change her mind. 'If we decided to go ahead with it, I mean.'

Charlie's eyebrows flew up as he took another sip of coffee. 'You want to?'

'I think it's not the worst idea the two of us have ever had when drunk.'

'No, that's still breaking in to see the new baby piglets on Mr Grange's farm when we were on our way home from the pub that night.' He shuddered. 'I still have nightmares about Momma Pig chasing us.'

'Agreed. This is definitely a better idea than that was.'

'But rules?' Charlie asked. 'What are you thinking?'

From the expression on his face, Millie knew he was already thinking his own way through the plan, spotting potential pitfalls and areas for which they'd need to have agreements in place.

'If the idea is to get married to have a family and be happy, we need to agree what that looks like for each of us,' she said, thinking it through as she spoke. 'Like fidelity.'

Charlie nodded vigorously. He knew how she felt about Tom's betrayal—and she knew how Octavia's cheating had almost broken him.

'Absolutely. If we're married, we're married. Properly and faithfully and all that. I don't want one of those marriages of convenience where it's all just for the name and the status, and secretly they're both carrying on with someone else on the side.'

Millie shuddered at the idea. 'Definitely not. So if we do this, we do it properly. The minute we say "I do" we're exclusive. What about sex?'

She tried, for a fleeting second, to imagine her and Charlie in bed together, and failed. All her brain would give her was images of Giles bloody Fairfax, which was *not* helpful.

What was the problem? Charlie was gorgeous, and she was sure any sex he had was good and fulfilling for both parties. It was just... he'd been her friend for too long for her to see him that way.

She'd have to get over that if they were getting married.

Sex with Charlie. Huh...

'My understanding is it's kind of essential for the having of children,' Charlie replied flippantly.

'Not necessarily.' Millie swallowed as she remembered her doctor's words. 'It might be that my fertility issues mean we need medical help anyway. There are options if you don't want...' She trailed off. She couldn't quite add *me*.

'That's not... It's not that I don't want...'

God, how were they going to do this if they couldn't even talk about it?

'I don't want a sexless marriage,' Charlie finished finally. 'If you're okay with that?'

'Yes. Of course.' She didn't want that either.

Even if the idea of her and Charlie in bed together still felt…alien.

Just because sex wasn't the number one priority in a marriage for her, it didn't mean she didn't want it. Should she be worried that the idea of sleeping with Charlie put her on edge? She certainly hadn't had that problem dancing with Giles the night before—something she was definitely blaming on the champagne.

Is it weird that it's never come up before?

All those years of friendship, nights spent together, her sleeping on that daybed. Was it strange that they'd never fallen into bed together before?

Of course before there had always been Octavia—or Tom, or someone else. Had they ever even been single at the same time before? She couldn't remember.

'So we're going to get married?' Even as she said it, she wasn't sure if it was a question or a statement.

'Great!'

Charlie smiled at her. She couldn't tell if it was the hangover or the subject matter that made it look…not quite right.

'That's… I mean… Happiest man alive and all that.'

'Charlie.' She reached over to take his hand. 'Keep being honest with me, okay?'

It was the only way they were going to get through this.

'I will make you a good husband,' he told her, suddenly serious. 'And a good father to our children. I think we can have a good marriage, Mills.'

And that was all she'd ever wanted. Wasn't it?

'Thank you.'

Suddenly, Charlie was all business. 'So, next steps. I guess we tell people. Time being of the essence baby-wise and all that.'

'Yes, I guess we do.'

She was going to have to tell her mother. She'd be thrilled, she was sure. But once Jessica Myles had the news, *everyone* would know, and there'd be no going back.

'Okay, then. There's a post-wedding meet-up at the pub. Let's start with Tabby and Giles.'

Giles. Of course Charlie was going to ask Giles to be his best man, just as Giles had predicted.

Millie couldn't help but be just the tiniest bit annoyed that this meant Giles had been right. On the other hand, she was going to get to spend the rest of her life with Charlie at her side. That meant that she'd won the endless battle of the best friends, didn't it?

And it was just as well she'd decided to put that sudden, ridiculous, out-of-the-blue crush on Giles out of her head. Because once she and Charlie were married, the chances were he'd be back in her life in a way he hadn't been since they were teenagers.

As a friend.

No more inappropriate thoughts at all, she told herself, firmly.

She couldn't afford them. Not if she was going to be Charlie's wife.

Giles woke up in his childhood bedroom, not hungover, but also not well rested. He'd spent the night tossing and turning as he thought over what he should have said to his sister, what he would say to his parents that morning, and everything else he'd ever done wrong in his life.

When he had slept, he'd dreamt of dancing. He hadn't been able to see his partner's face, because every time he'd tried to look she'd moved another step out of his reach, until he'd been dancing entirely alone.

Which, he reminded himself on waking, was only for the best.

His parents were already seated around the chilly breakfast table, eating cold eggs and burnt bacon, when he made his way to the dining room. Mrs Harper, the woman from the village who had sourly and unhappily been keeping the house ticking over and his parents fed for the last decade or more, scowled at him as he sat down, before stomping off towards the kitchen. If he was lucky, there might be some toast on its way.

'Giles. We weren't expecting you last night, were we?' His mother gave him an assessing look over her teacup.

'I was in the area,' he said vaguely. 'It was late. Seemed safer to stay here than risk driving back to London tired.'

'And here we were thinking you might have come to see your loving parents.' The edge in his father's voice was unmissable. 'Perhaps even take responsibility for this crumbling pile and the family fortunes. All this will be yours one day soon, you do realise!'

Quentin Fairfax flung his arms wide, the action violent enough to knock the arm of the chair next to him from its precarious hold on to the wooden chair-back and send it clattering to the ground.

'This whole place is falling apart,' Mrs Harper muttered as she reappeared, a plate of almost black toast in her hand.

'I'm not stopping long.' Giles looked at the toast and decided that there would be somewhere to stop for breakfast on his way home.

'You never do,' his mother said under her breath, and sent a glare at his father.

'Oh, and that's my fault, is it?' His father shoved his chair back and got to his feet. 'Of course it is. Everything always is, isn't it? No money? My fault. Never mind that our son has millions at his disposal and chooses to spend it elsewhere.'

'Well, maybe if you were a little more welcoming,' his mother shot back.

Giles looked between them and then stood up. They probably wouldn't even notice him leaving.

It took him no time at all to gather his things and get them back in the car. His mother caught up to him just as he slammed the boot.

'It really would help if you could just see to extending our allowance a little bit.' She wrapped her cardigan tighter around her. 'Your father would like to spend some money doing up the dining hall, for when we're entertaining.'

Of course he would.

His parents had no interest in learning how Giles had earned his money—the careful study, the networking and cultivating of working relationships with people in the field he wanted to be in, the stepping stones of jobs in the property investment company his mentor had owned, not to mention nearly a decade of working every hour God sent to be in the right position to take over the company when his mentor retired. That had made his career. His real money had come from studying the markets to learn about investing himself and taking the right kind of chances— not that he planned to tell his parents that part.

He wondered idly what Millie would make of all that if he told her. He knew what she thought of him—that he'd lucked out into a do-nothing job that paid well and lived off his inherited wealth the rest of the time. That was what he wanted people to believe, he supposed. In his circles there was something almost shameful about having to work hard for a living.

But Giles, despite his family name and advantages, had built his career himself. He'd earned his money himself. And he was damned if he was going to let his father fritter it away as if it were his right, without ever even asking where it came from.

He rested his hands on the door of his car and sighed. If he looked out to the east, he could see the village associated with the lands of the big manor house his parents still called home. A village they were supposed to look after and take care of, historically.

Supposed to being the most important words there.

'Wouldn't he rather use the money for fixing the roof? Or setting up a business to make the lodge self-financing instead of a giant money pit? Or even rebuilding the village hall after the fire last summer?' Giles couldn't help the edge in his voice.

'As I understand it, you've already taken care of the village hall,' his mother snapped back. 'You'll give *them* money, but not your own parents—'

'Because when Dad says "entertaining" he means more poker games, or buying more overpriced antiques he can't afford from friends who know he has no knowledge about these things.'

There was no way that Quentin Fairfax would change at this point in his life. For as long as Giles could remember his father had been spending money they didn't have on things they didn't need—then begging and borrowing for the essentials.

These days Giles paid for the essentials. But he wouldn't pay for any more.

He'd wait his father out. And when the lodge was his... Well...

Maybe then things would finally change.

God, he hoped so.

'I'll see you soon,' he told his mother, and drove away without looking back at her disapproving face in the rear-view mirror.

His phone rang as he pulled out onto the main road, already looking forward to returning to London. He connected the hands-free and answered.

'Giles? Are you still around, or have you gone back to London already?' Charlie's voice sounded tinny through the speakers.

'I'm still here,' he said. 'Just. What do you need?'

'Uh...could you come to The Fox and Duchess? Millie and I have something to ask you...'

CHAPTER FOUR

MILLIE HAD HOPED that the post-wedding meet-up at The Fox and Duchess would be small, and quiet—partly to facilitate her hangover recovery, but mostly because she and Charlie had a lot to talk about and she'd prefer not to have an audience. But this, like so many things lately, did not go to plan.

'The place is heaving!' Charlie pushed through the doors into the pub itself. 'See if you can grab us a table? I'll check they're still serving Sunday lunch.'

Millie made her way through the crowd, noting that the few remaining outside tables were also full. September was almost over, but some warmth still lingered here.

She didn't see the bride or groom—presumably they were already off on their honeymoon. But she spotted Charlie's sister Tabitha, holding court across the room with several of her friends, and waved.

Tabitha gave her a knowing look that suggested she knew exactly where Millie had spent last night. Charlie's sister had never bought their 'just friends' spiel.

Now they were about to prove her right.

She didn't admit to herself that she was looking for one face in particular until she realised he wasn't there. Charlie had called Giles on the way and asked him to meet them—she'd been right, he wanted to ask him to be best man. She should probably think about bridesmaids, too. There were so many things she suddenly had to think about.

She was getting *married*.

They hadn't told their families yet. Too many other things to work out first. But Charlie had assured her that, with all his best man experience, Giles would be able to help them make a plan to tackle it all. Millie wasn't convinced that best men were all that involved in planning anything more than the stag night, but he was their best option.

Well, no. The best option would be Tabitha, who worked in the family events business and had overseen hundreds of weddings, Millie was sure. But she also knew that the moment Tabitha was involved her wedding would suddenly be The Event of the Year, and that really wasn't what she wanted. Giles was more likely to just guide them through the basics.

But Giles wasn't there yet. And, as she slipped

into a tiny corner table just as the occupants were putting their coats on, Millie had to admit she was a little relieved about that. She still wasn't sure how much her sudden crush on him had been obvious at the wedding, and how embarrassed she should be.

Something tugged at her attention and she looked up, barely even surprised when she realised that Giles had entered the pub and was scanning the room, looking for them. His gaze caught hers and locked, and once again she felt that strange connection she'd tried to ignore on the dance floor.

'Millie. Charlie at the bar?' Giles slid into the seat opposite her, leaving the extra chair on the side for Charlie. 'He asked me to meet you guys here.'

'I know.' Millie swallowed. 'He... Well, he'll explain when he gets here.'

She could see the curiosity in Giles's eyes, but he didn't press. He gave her a small, tight smile, but he didn't mention the night before at all. Maybe he really hadn't noticed. That would be something.

Charlie had told her he'd warned Giles off her, but she was certain that was just Giles winding Charlie up. This was further proof.

'Giles! You made it.' Charlie swept up to the table and deposited drinks between them. 'Thanks so much for coming.'

Giles broke away from Millie's gaze to smile at Charlie. 'Of course! So, what's so urgent it couldn't wait until next time we meet up in London? I *had* planned to try and avoid this shindig altogether, now the bride's out of the country and can't order me about any more.'

'Well…' Charlie glanced nervously at Millie and reached out to take her hand. But before he could get any further, another figure barged up to their table.

'Charlie! And Giles! The old gang back together!'

Millie's jaw tightened as she recognised Ronan, an old schoolfriend of Charlie's—not one she'd ever liked.

Charlie, meanwhile, liked everybody. 'Ronan! Good to see you, buddy. You weren't at the wedding yesterday, were you?'

'Not me, mate. I don't reach Octavia's exacting standards. But I wanted to come and catch up with you all anyway.' Ronan lowered his tone, although he still spoke loudly enough for the whole pub to hear. 'And to see how you're coping, of course. Can't be easy…watching the love of your life marrying another. Bet you went home and had a little cry last night, didn't you?'

That was Ronan all over—pretending to be friends and then needling in the back, digging and cutting and causing pain. And Millie couldn't bear it.

'Actually, he went home with me.' She placed a hand over Charlie's and smiled up at him in what she hoped was a loving fiancée way. 'You see, we just got engaged last night.'

Giles managed to swallow the mouthful of his pint rather than spitting it out at Millie's announcement—which he was calling a win.

Married? Millie and Charlie? Now?

Yes, he'd hinted at it to them both the night before—even as he'd flirted with Millie while they danced. But he hadn't expected them to go from not-a-couple to *engaged* in the space of twelve hours. Hadn't they heard of dating?

He considered the idea that Millie was only saying it to annoy Ronan, but Charlie was nodding. And in the hushed silence that followed he saw Tabitha streaking across the room towards them, wide eyed.

'What?' She slammed to a halt beside their table. 'Did I just hear that right? Have you two *finally* got your heads out of your—?'

'Tabby,' Charlie interrupted, but she carried on regardless.

'Out of your you-know-whats and decided to do something about the *obvious* fact that the two of you are in love with each other?'

Charlie and Millie exchanged a look, and Giles realised he was holding his breath, waiting for an answer.

'If you're asking if we're engaged to be married,' Charlie said slowly. 'Then the answer is yes.'

Tabitha's squeal almost burst Giles's eardrums. He wasn't sure he'd mind. He'd quite like to be deaf at this point, then he wouldn't have to hear this news.

I should be happy for them. This is perfect for both of them. Hell, I even suggested it.

So why did it feel as if his stomach had sunk through the floor the moment Millie said the words?

'This is just *perfect!*' Tabitha leaned over to hug Millie, then Charlie, then Millie again. 'And you must be the best man again Giles, then?' She hugged him, too, then stepped back to give him an appraising look. She leaned in to stage whisper, 'Millie, if you're in need of a maid of honour, I definitely wouldn't mind standing up with him. Or not standing up, if you get my meaning.'

'*Tabby.*'

Charlie looked genuinely pained by his sister's antics. Giles wondered how long she'd been in the pub.

'No, you see, the *reason* it's perfect is that we've just had a cancellation for a Christmas Eve wedding up at the house!' Tabby bounced on her toes as she clasped her hands together in genuine joy. 'Because you *are* getting married at the house, right?'

'Oh, of course…' Millie said, sounding uncertain.

Giles was almost certain she'd never even thought about it.

'And Millie! You've always wanted a Christmas wedding, haven't you?'

'I have?'

She seemed even more uncertain about that. Giles suspected that *Tabby* had always wanted Millie to have a Christmas wedding, which wasn't quite the same thing.

'Of course! With your colouring, jewel tones and a winter theme will be *perfect* for you.' Tabby clapped her hands again. 'I'm going to go up to the office and book you in now, before anyone else can steal your date. Mum and Dad are going to be so excited!'

She hurried off, presumably to spread the news like a slightly tipsy town crier in a floral dress. Her brother chased after her, presumably to temper exactly what she was going to tell their parents.

Most people watched them go.

Giles watched Millie.

'A Christmas wedding, huh?' he asked.

'Apparently.' She smiled, but the slightly blindsided look Tabby's announcement had given her didn't fade. 'I mean, I thought we were talking about next year, but actually… Christmas will be perfect.'

'Once you find the person you want to spend the rest of your life with you want the rest of your life to start right away—that sort of thing? Very *When Harry met Sally.*'

As was the proof that perhaps men and women couldn't be just friends after all. He and Millie had certainly never managed it.

But they'd have to now, if she was marrying Charlie.

Except last night they'd both denied there was anything more than friendship between them. And now they were getting married? It all seemed rather...sudden.

Even though he'd kept those thoughts to himself, Millie had obviously intuited that he was thinking them.

'I know this must be a bit of a surprise.' She bit her lower lip. 'To be honest, it came as a bit of a surprise to us, too.'

'You didn't fancy dating first?' He said it as a joke, although it wasn't...not really. 'Most people do.'

'I guess we realised that, actually, we'd been dating for years,' she said with a smile. 'We go out together, we spend quiet nights in together, we talk every day and we're always each other's plus one for things these days.'

'That sounds like a great friendship,' Giles said cautiously. 'But marriage is a little bit more.'

'Is it?' She raised her eyebrows questioningly.

'Surely friendship is the basis of any good marriage.'

'But what about…?' He wasn't going to say sex. He wasn't going to be That Guy, who brought everything down to its basest level.

But at the same time…what *about* sex?

Friendship was one thing—he had friends; he knew that. Maybe not as close and as caring as Charlie and Millie had always been, but still. He had friends. And he didn't want to sleep with any of them.

'Passion,' he finished, the memory of holding her in his arms as they danced returning with a vengeance.

'You mean sex?'

Her cheeks flushed a deeper pink as she said it. He had to admit, it was adorable.

'Do you really think that's the most important thing in a marriage?'

'No,' he admitted.

He'd never asked his sister and brother-in-law or his parents about their sex life, but even if it was good their clashing personalities and expectations still made them miserable. It wasn't that he couldn't see Millie's point…

'But it does matter.'

He wasn't going to get married. But if he was, he would want it to be to someone he had a physical connection with. Someone who could turn him on with a glance…who he wanted to touch all the time.

He met Millie's gaze and felt his body start to warm, so he looked away again. Fast.

'Charlie and I…' Millie glanced down at the table, her cheeks redder than ever. 'We've never been single at the same time before, so we never had time to explore that side of things. Until now.'

Suddenly it all made sense to Giles.

This was all his fault.

He'd got them thinking about each other in a romantic light at the wedding yesterday, then sent them off tipsy together, and they'd promptly acted on his suggestion and fallen into bed together.

And apparently that physical connection he wanted was so strong between them that they'd decided to cut out the faffing around of dating and just get married straight away.

Millie was right. They already had one of the strongest friendships he knew. They knew each other inside out. Add in a fantastic sex life and, really, what else was there? They probably had the best shot at a happy marriage of anyone he'd ever met.

And if a small part of him wished that, now they were adults instead of bickering teens, he'd had a shot with Millie before they figured that out…? Well, he was going to shout that down. Because he couldn't give Millie the happy-ever-after life she wanted anyway, and she and Charlie both deserved this.

'I'm happy for you both,' he said.

And he almost completely meant it.

Millie should have known that as soon as Tabby had heard the news the rest of the family would, too and they'd be summoned up to Howard Hall. At least she'd had a little time to practise being convincingly in love with Charlie beforehand. She was *almost* sure that Giles had bought it.

After all, it made sense. That was why they were doing it.

But it mattered, suddenly, to Millie that people believed they were doing it for the right reasons—and she knew that, as solid as the reasons she and Charlie had were to them, other people might not agree.

Other people like her mum.

'Millie!' Jessica Myles was waiting on the steps of Howard Hall, her arms spread wide, ready to welcome her daughter to what would, after her marriage, be her new home.

Oh, God. I hadn't thought about that.

Howard Hall was *enormous.* And historic. And imposing. It was one thing to stay there in Charlie's rooms now and then. But to *live* there?

'I can't believe it!' Her mum was still hugging her. Tightly. 'We always hoped… But obviously the heart wants what the heart wants. You never really know. And Charlie has always been so sweet to you… I'm so happy for you! I just wish your father was here to see it.'

'Me too, Mum.'

That was easy to agree with. The rest…

Nobody—in her family or Charlie's—had ever said out loud that they thought the two of them should be more than friends. But, from the way Charlie's parents were beaming down at them from the front door, it seemed she might just be enough of a better option than Charlie not marrying at all for everyone to be happy.

Even if she never *really* felt she belonged, her children would, and that was what mattered.

Children. She was going to have a family with her best friend. That was what she needed to focus on here.

They were all ushered inside, where Millie was welcomed with hugs from all the members of Charlie's family and sherry was poured all round. Millie tried to keep her hungover stomach in order as she smiled and accepted hers.

'To Charlie and Millie!'

The toast echoed around the room and Millie's head pounded as their drunken idea took full form.

'What happened to Giles?' Charlie asked, as everyone talked at once about their wedding plans. 'I never got around to asking him to be best man.'

'He stayed to settle up at the bar,' she said. 'For us and for Tabby and Liberty. You kind of ran off in a hurry.'

'That's why he's going to be best man,' Charlie said, with a grin. 'He's good at taking care of things like that.'

'Now, Millie, have you thought about your wedding gown yet?' Lady Howard asked.

Charlie's Aunt Felicity burst in before Millie could answer.

'She should wear Mother's! Although it might need to be let out a bit,' she added, eyeing Millie as if she was one of her prized horses.

'No way,' Tabby said, shaking her head in a way that just reminded Millie of how her own head still ached. 'Millie's going to want something new—something *her*. Ooh, can I come wedding dress shopping with you? We can have our own *Say Yes To The Dress* moment!'

'Maybe…' Millie hedged.

'What about the ring?' Charlie's father asked. 'You didn't ask for the family one to propose with.'

Millie's heart clenched. Did they suspect? Had they all figured out that this wasn't a love match? She wanted them to believe it was real. It made it easier for her to pretend it was, too.

'Because Mother is still wearing it,' Charlie pointed out drily. 'And I want Millie to have a ring that *she* loves, so we'll pick one out together.'

He squeezed her hand as he said it, and it should have made her feel reassured. Loved. Instead it just reminded her that buying a ring was one more thing to do before their Christmas Eve wedding date.

Oh, God. How was she even going to do it all? She had her own floristry business to run, and it wasn't as if Christmas was a quiet time of year, with all the wreaths and garlands and the festive flower workshops she ran from her little shop.

She just wanted to be *married.* This whole wedding business was just getting in the way.

Luckily, everyone else seemed to be happy to get on with organising it without her. The planning conversation was now exclusively between Tabby and their mothers, with Aunt Felicity adding an occasional unhelpful comment. Charlie's father was beckoning him over towards the drinks cabinet, so Millie took the opportunity to escape for a moment.

'I'll go see if Giles is here yet,' she murmured, before slipping out into the hall.

As soon as she was certain she wasn't being followed, she darted towards the front door and out into the crisp autumn air.

She hadn't really planned to look for Giles—that had just been a convenient excuse to escape the suffocating air in that room. But as she stood with her back against the ancient door she saw him making his way up the long driveway on foot. He must have left his car at the pub, she realised. It was quicker to walk between Howard Hall and The Fox and Duchess than to drive, given the twisty Norfolk roads, and there was a shortcut over the fields that she and Charlie had been exploiting since they were teenagers.

She knew the moment he spotted her, because there was a slight hitch in his steps, and she felt her heart give a double beat before he carried on towards her.

'Running away already?' Giles asked, pausing as he approached the bottom of the steps.

Millie smiled and shook her head. 'Just needed some air. Hangover.'

'Right.' Giles tilted his head as he studied her. 'They can be a bit much, I know. Families.'

'I love Charlie's family,' she objected. 'And my own mum is in there, too.'

'Still.' He shrugged. 'People get crazy about weddings. Don't feel you have to give in to everything they want. It's your special day, after all. You and Charlie love each other, and you get to choose how you share that with your guests.'

'Is that your accumulated best man wisdom?' she asked.

'Basically. That and don't forget that a wedding is only one day. A marriage is the rest of your life.'

Somehow he managed to make the words

sound like a ball and chain, clamping around her ankle.

'That's the idea,' she said, as brightly as she could. 'Come on. There's sherry inside.'

Even the wedding planning conversations were more appealing than this.

CHAPTER FIVE

IT WASN'T THAT Millie was trying not to think about her impending wedding. But it *was* surprisingly easy to push it to the back of her mind when she was engrossed in her work. Back in her little florist shop in a small village outside London, somewhere between the capital and Howard Hall in Norfolk, where she belonged.

At least until her phone rang and she saw Charlie's name on the screen, and she felt her chest tighten.

Normally they'd text each other through the day, but the last week had been silent between them. As if they were both still processing the momentous change in their relationship that was coming.

But now Charlie was calling.

She swiped to answer. 'Hey.'

'Hey, is this a bad time?'

It was weird how he still sounded just like her best friend, not her fiancé.

'No, no. I'm just designing the colours for that

pitch—you know the big corporate event I mentioned?'

Back when things were normal.

'How's it going?' Charlie asked.

'Hmm, not quite there. It feels a little brassy at the moment. They want glamour, but classy glamour—diamonds not rhinestones, you know?'

And it didn't help that she kept getting distracted, thinking about her own wedding flowers—if she could figure out what she wanted for them, everything else would fall into place.

'Do they want Christmassy colours?'

'Yes, but not traditional. So red and white are out, which makes things tricky. I'll get there. I've just been distracted.'

From the brief silence that followed, he knew exactly by what.

'We've just had the weekly meeting and there's an opportunity to let out Glenmere Castle for a couple of months, starting now,' he said, after a moment.

Millie blinked at the abrupt change in topic. 'Erm…that's good.' She'd lost track of quite how many properties Charlie's family owned and ran. That was probably something else she should figure out before they got married.

'For a film shoot. Liberty is the location manager—you know, Tabby's friend. She's had a crisis. A flood or something. Anyway, we're stepping in and offering her the venue.'

He was babbling. That was never a good sign.

'Okay…' She waited. Eventually he'd tell her what was really going on.

'Anyway, we're not quite set up for letting yet. Still snagging and so on. So the only way we could agree is if one of us is on site for the shoot.'

Or maybe he didn't need to tell her. She could already tell exactly what was coming next.

'By "one of us" you mean you?'

He was going to Scotland. Now. Leaving her here to deal with…everything else.

'I know the timing is horrible…'

Was she supposed to laugh or cry at this? She wasn't sure.

'We are supposed to be getting married in less than three months, Charlie, and are you seriously telling me you are heading off to Scotland for the entire duration, with everything still to plan?'

'Is this our first marital disagreement?'

If it was an attempt at a joke, it was a bad one. She could practically hear him wincing.

'Mum and Tabby seem to have everything in hand…'

That was what made her feelings start to boil over. Charlie was delegating their *wedding* to his mother and sister.

'But this is *our* wedding! I don't want to be steamrollered by your family. It might not be the most traditional of set-ups, but that doesn't mean it shouldn't be meaningful…personal. If things go the way we plan, then this will be the only wedding either of us have.'

There was a pause, and when Charlie spoke again there were no more excuses. 'I'm sorry, Millie. I'm an arse. I didn't think. You're right. I'll tell Tabby we can't accommodate the booking after all...'

Her anger faded in an instant.

'Is that the alternative?' She sighed. 'I don't want you to lose out. I'm being silly. It's just a little overwhelming, you know?'

'I really do,' Charlie said, with feeling. 'Look, Giles is around. How about I get him to stand in for me on any wedding-related business? I'll be at the end of the phone whenever you need a decision, and he can be there for all the tastings and whatnot, so that you're not alone and at my family's mercy. He's my best man after all. Let's make him earn it.'

'Giles. Right.'

Ideal. Just what she needed. But she could hardly tell Charlie that, could she? Either he'd think she was holding on to a childhood grudge, or she'd have to admit that she'd had some entirely *non*-childish thoughts about him since they'd danced together at Octavia's wedding.

'If I was marrying anyone else I would want you, obviously, but I think juggling the roles of best woman and bride is too much, don't you?' Charlie joked.

She laughed. 'True! Look, of course you should go. I'll manage. No one is indispensable—not even the groom.'

'That's what Mum and Tabby think. They think I am completely surplus to requirements.'

He didn't sound as if he minded too much.

'They're just excited for us. It's nice.'

At least, that was what she kept telling herself.

'It is.'

Another pause. Millie could hear the wind in the trees down the line. He must be outside.

'Are you?' he asked suddenly.

'Am I what?'

'Excited for us?'

Millie considered her answer. She wasn't going to start lying to her best friend—her future husband—now. That wouldn't bode well for marriage, would it?

Finally, she said, 'I'm excited to get started with our lives. I kind of wish we could fast forward through the engagement and wedding part, though.'

'We could fly to Vegas tonight.'

She almost believed he meant it.

'Is that what you want?' she asked.

It was Charlie's turn to fall silent for a long moment. Then, 'Mother would never forgive me—nor would yours. And I know better than to upset the cook. Look, Millie…'

'Mmm?'

'I'm going to be gone for a while.'

'I know.'

Where was he going with this?

'I meant what I said about fidelity, but we're not actually married yet. So, look, what happens in Vegas stays in Vegas. I'm fine with that.'

Vegas? What?

'Charlie, what on *earth* are you babbling about? I thought we decided not to go to Vegas?'

'I mean, if you want a final fling or two, or whatever, before you say *I do,* then you should go for it. Sow those wild oats, as my grandfather used to say.'

Wild oats. Really?

'A final fling? Charlie, I have never had a fling in my life!'

And it was definitely not a good thing that the first person she thought of when she said those words was Giles Fairfax, of all people.

This was why passion was dangerous. She might be attracted to Giles, but that kind of chemistry only led to heartbreak when it wore off. She needed something more long term than a passing fancy.

'So maybe you should, while you can,' Charlie said, a little too eagerly for her liking.

'Hang on, is this about you?' Her voice sharpened. 'Are *you* having regrets? Do *you* want to be sowing oats?'

'Me? No. I'll be in the wilds of Scotland.'

'With an entire film crew and no doubt several eligible actresses. It's not as if you'll be a hermit in a bothy,' she pointed out. 'I'm sure there will be enough women for several flings. An entire magic porridge pot of wild oats.'

'I didn't mean it like that… I'm not interested in actresses or anyone. Honestly, Mills, this isn't me saying I want to sleep with someone before settling down with you. I've never actually had a fling either.'

Of course he hadn't. It had always been Octavia for him. And now it was her.

'Then maybe you *should* do some sowing, too. Maybe you're right. We are about to commit to each other for life. Maybe we should…oh, I don't know…not go out there *looking* for a fling, but not feel guilty if the opportunity comes up. Argh! I can't believe I just said that—but do I mean it?'

She thought. Probably. But she *definitely* wasn't thinking about Giles as she said it. He, of all people, was not an option.

'Okay, then. This is weird. Isn't this weird?'

'A little,' she admitted. 'But we've always been able to talk about anything before. I think it's important we still do. And I think, with you gone for two months or so and the wedding so close, you're right. This is our last time to…you know… act on pure attraction rather than being sensible.'

'Millie Myles. Are you saying you're not attracted to me?'

And there, of course, was the biggest concern she had about this whole thing. She'd just never thought of Charlie that way.

But that's a good thing. I'm looking for a marriage that lasts, *and that means it can't be based on passion.*

She and Charlie had something better than that. And she had to have faith that the rest would come—at least enough for them to be content with it. Deep, real respect and love was far more important than sex.

'I'm working on it.'

She laughed, but it didn't feel funny. Loving Charlie was easy. It was everything else that was a leap of faith.

'We'll get there,' he promised. 'Okay, let me break the glad news to Giles…'

Millie's chest tightened again. 'You're going to tell *Giles* that we're allowed to sleep with someone else while we're engaged?'

'No! He believes he has played Cupid, and who I am to dissuade him? I'm going to let him know that his best man duties have expanded somewhat. You're okay with that? I know you and he can be a little off, but he's a good sort when you get to know him.'

'Yes. Of course. Look… I'd better go—this colour scheme won't resolve itself. Bye, Charlie.'

She hung up before she could hear his answer.

Then she looked at the designs she'd been working on, put her head on her arms and groaned.

Planning a wedding with Giles Fairfax. This was going to be a disaster.

It was easy enough, back in London, for Giles to put the events of Octavia's wedding and the days that had followed from his head. Well, mostly.

Charlie had asked him to be best man, as expected—but, given that Tabby and the mothers of the bride and groom seemed to have all the wedding planning in hand, and Charlie didn't want an extravagant stag do, it seemed likely that all Giles would need to do was show up on the day with the rings, an appropriate speech, and a willingness to usher difficult relatives into place with a charming smile.

He could do all that standing on his head by this point.

No, Charlie's Christmas Eve wedding looked to be the easiest one he'd had to take part in yet.

Even if the idea of him marrying *Millie* still made something in his chest tighten if he thought about it for too long...

So Giles happily threw himself back into his old life—into work and drinks with colleagues, business dinners and early-morning breakfast meetings, and nothing even slightly wedding-related.

Until Charlie called and told him he had a little addition to his best man duties.

'I'm sorry, what?' Giles must have heard him wrong. That was the only possible explanation here. 'You need me to…what?'

'Help Millie with the wedding.'

Charlie was on hands-free in his car, and Giles could hear the traffic and the wind whistling by outside.

'I've got to go to Scotland for the next ten weeks or so, to oversee a production up at Glenmere. For insurance reasons. Can't get out of it. But I don't want Millie to be left to Tabby's tender care when it comes to all the wedding planning either. So could you just…help out? If she needs it?'

'You're going to Scotland for over two months. Right before your wedding.' Giles still wasn't quite sure he was hearing this right. 'And Millie is okay with this?'

There was a telling silence on the other end before Charlie replied, 'She understands. It's the family business. There's no one else who can do it.'

'Still…' Giles couldn't imagine any of the other brides he'd known going along with this plan.

'Besides, you know that my input is the least important. It'll be Millie and Tabby and our mothers organising the whole thing, anyway.'

'Right…'

There was something odd here, but Giles couldn't put his finger on quite what it was. Charlie *was* unnaturally dedicated to the family business. And, God knew, Giles understood work commitments that were impossible to get out of—another reason, if he needed one, why a long-lasting relationship wasn't on the cards for him.

'So what do you need *me* to do?'

If the women were taking charge, surely he was surplus to requirements?

'Just…be there for Millie.'

Charlie sounded faintly guilty, Giles realised. Well, good. So he should. Not for putting this on him, but for abandoning Millie right now.

'Don't let Tabby and the others steamroller her into a wedding she doesn't want. I want… I really want this to be her perfect day.'

'Not yours?' Giles asked.

'If it's perfect for her, it's perfect for me. Just make sure she gets everything she wants, right?'

Ah, so this was how Charlie was salving his conscience over leaving—throwing money at the problem. Giles could relate. Even if, with his own family, he'd chosen the opposite path.

'I'll do everything I can,' he promised. 'Send me her contact details so I can get in touch.'

After they'd hung up, Giles tried to throw himself back into his work, but his focus was shot, and his assistants had already left, so he decided to call it a night. Checking his phone, he saw a new contact card from Charlie, that had Millie's phone number, email and address.

Holly and Ivy Florists

Her shop. He'd never visited it before, but the address showed it was in a village outside London, off to the north-east. Probably in the commuter belt, but still only an hour or so from Charlie's home, Howard Hall, in Norfolk.

He wondered if she'd keep it after the wedding, or if she'd throw her floral talents into the Howard family business.

Maybe he'd ask her.

Maybe he'd ask her how she felt about her fiancé disappearing right before their wedding while he was at it. Try to smooth the ground for Charlie there.

Before he could second-guess himself, he grabbed his car keys and headed down to the office's underground car park. He'd made a promise to his best friend and he intended to keep it.

Weddings, it turned out, were bigger business than Millie had thought.

Oh, she'd done enough wedding flowers in her time to know how extravagant they could get, how expensive, and how utterly obsessed some people could become with planning the perfect wedding. She'd seen the beautiful venues, the stunning gowns, the fabulous catering, the three different photographers and the videographer all trying not to get in each other's shots.

But what she hadn't realised was just how many decisions there were to make.

She'd visited her local library and taken out a couple of wedding planning books, as well as bookmarking the top websites recommended in all the wedding magazines Tabitha had handed her before she'd left Howard Hall. Every single one of them promised to give her the *only* checklist she needed to plan her wedding—except every checklist had different things on it. And that was even before she got to the email she'd received from Tabby the moment she'd returned home to her little flat above the florist's shop in the village of Wendon Stye.

Now, as she sighed at the stack of wedding-related publications sitting on her tiny coffee table, she pulled the email up again on her phone.

Hi Millie!
Just checking in about the first things we need to sort for the wedding. Numbers are obviously the big one, so I'm attaching the guest list from our side. You know Charlie will never do it, but you'll need to check with him about friends and colleagues he wants to invite in addition to these,

so you can add your lot on, too and we'll see how it all shakes out.

The attached guest list had almost given her a heart attack. There were almost two hundred names on it, before she and Charlie even talked about who *they* wanted there.

But that wasn't the end of the email.

Let me know when you want to go dress shopping—I've got some great contacts who can find or design you something truly unique, even in our condensed timeframe. And I know you'll want to take care of the flowers, but let's talk about your colour scheme soon, so I can start sourcing the other decorations and table-ware, etc.

I'm also attaching our usual list of recommended suppliers for music for the ceremony and bands for the evening. Oh, and our current seasonal menus, although these will change once we get the Christmas menus confirmed. We'll arrange a date for you to come up and do the tasting for that, and the wine...

I've block-booked as much local accommodation as I can for now, so guests can reserve what they need when they confirm their acceptance. Other things—like timings for the day and plans for the evening, etc.—can wait a little while, but not too long as we'll want to put details on the invitations.

Oh, speaking of which! Here are a couple of examples from stationers we've used recently for you to take a look at. Classic and refined, of course.

I think that's all for now! Can't wait to get started.

Love

Tabby x

PS Here's the wedding checklist I give to all our Howard Hall brides. The only list you'll need!

Tabby's checklist, Millie noted, had twice as many items on it as any of the other ones she'd found. She'd printed it out on the office printer downstairs and almost run out of paper.

With a sigh, she slumped back down onto her sofa and dropped her phone onto the cushions. She'd have to start going through it all soon, but right now it just felt too overwhelming.

If only Charlie was there to do it with her. Then they could laugh at all these ridiculous requirements, and how they didn't care about any of this stuff, telling each other it was just another hoop to jump through before they could get on with what they actually wanted to do—living a happy family life together, as best friends.

But Charlie was away in Scotland, overseeing Liberty's movie at Glenmere Castle, and wouldn't be back until right before the wedding. It was unavoidable, he'd assured her, but that didn't stop her worrying. Did he regret their decision to marry? Was he looking for a way out already?

If he was, she needed him to tell her now—before she fell down Tabby's wedding-planning rabbit hole.

So she asked—outright. That was another advantage of marrying her best friend rather than a romantic partner. She had no qualms about confronting him about things because he couldn't break her heart. Although he could take away her future…and if he was going to do it she'd rather he do it now than later.

But Charlie assured her he was still all in.

'This is what I want, Mills,' he said firmly. 'That isn't going to change. But I just need… I need to be in Scotland right now. I promise you I'll be back.'

And she trusted him, so she knew he would be.

Just not in time to do any of this damn wedding planning.

Downstairs, the doorbell rang, and she frowned. The shop had been closed for hours, and there was no flower-arranging workshop scheduled for tonight. She hadn't ordered any takeaway, and Charlie was in Scotland.

Millie had literally no idea who else might be calling on her here at the shop.

Pulling a fluffy cardigan over her pyjamas,

she plodded down the creaky wooden stairs in her slippers and peered out through a gap in the closed blinds.

A tall figure stood outside, wearing a long, black woollen coat, a mobile phone clamped to his ear.

In her cardigan pocket, her own phone started to ring.

The man turned as she fumbled to answer it, the sound of her sleigh bell ringtone obviously sounding through the glass.

It's October now. That's nearly *Christmas, right? Sleigh bells are totally acceptable.*

He smirked, and his features came into focus. *Giles Fairfax.*

What the hell was he doing here?

Ending the call, she yanked open the door. 'We're closed, you realise?'

'This isn't a business visit.'

Giles stepped inside and she shuffled backwards out of his way, leaving him to shut the door and lock it again behind him.

'Charlie sent me to help.'

'Of course he did.'

When Charlie had said that Giles would help, she'd assumed it would be with things like addressing invitations or something. Not showing up at her flat unannounced one evening when she was already in her pyjamas.

Charlie didn't trust her to organise this wedding, so he'd sent his best man to babysit her. Because Giles, of course, knew everything there was to know about society weddings. He'd been born into that world and, by all accounts, had spent far more time involved in making them happen for his friends over the last few years than anyone else they knew.

It made perfect sense. It also made acid rise in her throat and caused her to want to throw things.

'Okay, from that glower I'm guessing that this is not a welcome intervention?' Giles pulled a bottle of Prosecco from behind his back. 'Does this help? I realised I hadn't actually bought you an engagement present yet.'

'It's a start,' Millie allowed.

Then she sighed. He'd obviously travelled up after work, since he was still wearing his suit— and, while it wasn't a *very* long drive, it still took a lot to get Giles and his sort to leave the capital, in her experience. And, since he'd already en- joyed the sight of her in her fuzzy slippers and pyjamas combo, there wasn't much point send- ing him away.

Also, if she knew Giles Fairfax at all—which she didn't, much, but she knew enough men like him—the Prosecco would be of the highest qual- ity. And she really could do with a glass.

'Oh, all right then,' she said. 'Come on up to Wedding Planning Central.'

CHAPTER SIX

GILES HADN'T EVER visited the village of Wendon Stye before tonight, but from what he'd seen driving through it in the falling darkness it was much like many picturesque English villages outside the M25. With a grassy area in the centre with the war memorial, a church rather larger than he suspected the current congregation warranted, some thatched and beamed cottages in the centre, and lots more recently built terraced and semi-detached houses radiating outwards on the new estates.

Millie's florist shop, Holly and Ivy, had a prime position on the small high street, between boutique interiors shops and organic cafés. Clearly Wendon Stye was catering to high-earning professionals and their families—the ones who'd moved out of London when they started having kids, but with one or both parents still commuting the hour or so back in, to be able to afford to live there or pay school fees.

It was a village for families.

Giles had wrapped his coat tighter around himself and hoped no local curtain twitchers would notice how much he didn't belong there.

Millie, when she had appeared to let him in, had looked both surprised and annoyed to see him. Not counting Octavia's wedding and the following day, Giles hadn't seen Millie more than a handful of times since he and Charlie had left school. He'd stopped visiting for a week every summer holiday. And he'd certainly never seen her in pyjamas with fuzzy pink slippers on her feet.

Not that it mattered. He still felt that same surge of attraction he'd discovered while dancing with her at the wedding, even knowing how incredibly inappropriate it was. Hopefully she didn't notice the way he kept a Victorian-era-level respectable distance between them. It was just that he couldn't shake the worry that if his hand brushed against her skin there might be actual sparks.

The shop was in darkness as she led him through it, although the scent of flowers and fresh greenery still filled the air, and he saw the occasional holly berry gleaming red in the flashes of light from the streetlamp outside. He followed Millie through a back door behind the counter, then up a staircase that creaked as badly as the one at Fairfax Manor, to a bijou flat above the shop.

He'd never really imagined where Millie might live, but if he had, he suspected he wouldn't have included quite so many cushions and throws in his vision. Every inch of the bright, sunny yellow sofa seemed to be covered with them, almost running into the deep pile rug that filled most of the wooden floor.

The small coffee table in front of the sofa—the only table there was space for in the whole living area—was also covered, this time in bridal magazines, printouts from wedding websites and invitation samples.

'Wedding planning going well, then?'

'Wedding planning is…' Millie sighed. 'Give me the Prosecco.' She headed for the kitchen area he could just see through an open door, calling back over her shoulder, 'You can sit! Just…move things.'

Giles considered his options, then shifted a stack of magazines from the armchair next to the sofa onto the floor beside the coffee table and sat. By the time Millie returned with a champagne flute full of Prosecco for him, he was already flicking through the checklist he'd spotted on top of the magazines.

'Tabby's work, I assume?' He waved the checklist at her.

'Oh, yeah. Apparently a lot more goes into planning a wedding than I ever imagined.'

Millie dropped down into a small gap between

cushions and paperwork on the sofa, her own glass in hand.

'Looks like it.'

The checklist ran to several pages, and was ordered into different sections by headings in a curly font. Each item had a heart-shaped check box next to it.

He tossed the list back on the table. 'This is why Charlie sent me, you realise?'

Okay, maybe *sent* was a little strong, but he'd asked him to help, and this was the only way Giles could think of to do that. Besides, looking at the wedding chaos that had taken over Millie's home, he hadn't arrived a moment too soon.

'He didn't want Tabby to take over your wedding and strong-arm you into things you don't want. He trusts *you* to organise your wedding, not his sister. So I'm here to help you do that.'

Millie's shoulders seemed to straighten a little at that. 'That's really why he sent you?'

'Why else?'

She gave a small shrug, but he read sentences into it.

'You thought he didn't trust you to organise a society wedding on your own, didn't you?' he realised.

'It's not entirely ridiculous,' Millie said. 'It's not like I have a lot of experience with this sort of thing. Unlike you.'

It was funny, Giles thought. Ever since he'd

met Charlie, back at school, he'd heard about his best friend Millie. The brave, funny, unstoppable Millie. The one person who meant more to Charlie than anyone—except possibly his actual family.

As a child, he'd been jealous of her before he'd even met her. She held a place in Charlie's life that he could never touch. And a place in the world that he couldn't imagine.

He didn't know how much of the Millie of his imagination was real, but back then he'd assumed she had everything that he didn't. She was part of Charlie's happy home life, with its successful family, and buildings that weren't crumbling around them, and parents who didn't argue all the time. He knew, sort of, that she wasn't *really* a part of it—that she lived in the gatehouse and her own parents worked for Charlie's. But as a young boy that distinction hadn't been as clear as it had become when he grew up. If anything, it had just added to his impression that Millie had both the freedom and the acceptance that he never expected to have.

It had been a year or so into his friendship with Charlie before his first invitation to Howard Hall, during the summer break. Even then, he'd been unsure about visiting—because to do so would require him to invite Charlie to Fairfax Manor in return, and he'd already known he couldn't do *that*. And until that first visit Millie had remained the perfect friend, who had a relationship with Charlie that he'd always wanted.

Giles was ashamed to admit he'd hated her a little then.

By the time they'd met, that view had been fairly ingrained. Most of the time he'd kept his distance—and she'd kept hers during his visits, too. When they *had* met, they'd clashed—often spectacularly.

Soon enough he'd realised how imperfect her position was—and the huge advantages his own life had given him, even if they didn't always feel that way. But he'd never expected to feel *sorry* for Millie until this very moment. Seeing her so uncertain about her own place in the world made him want to tear down anyone and any thing that made her feel that way. To turn a mirror on her and show her what *he* saw. A gorgeous, kind, incredible woman.

He was man enough to admit that now. Because they weren't vying to be Charlie's best friend any longer. That battle was over—she was his fiancée, going to be his wife, and Giles would still be his best friend and that was enough for him.

Maybe they could *all* be friends. He hoped so.

And it started here, with him helping her with this wedding, just as Charlie had asked.

He could do that.

He just couldn't let himself get distracted by how absurdly cute she looked with her hair piled on top of her head and an oversized cardigan wrapped around her. Or how much he *still* wanted to peel that cardigan off her and find out what was underneath…

Not what you're here for, Fairfax.

'This is *your* wedding,' he said firmly. 'Yours and Charlie's. Everything else—tradition, society's expectations, keeping other people happy—that has to come afterwards. Make sure you've got what you really want—the things that matter to you and Charlie—and *then* let Tabby in to add her own sparkle to the things that don't matter so much to you.'

Millie blinked at him with obvious surprise. 'That's…actually really good advice.'

'Of course it is.' Giles was only *slightly* offended. 'Weddings are just like business negotiations, really. You have to know what matters to you before you go into the room. Unless you're a real Bridezilla—and I'm not suggesting you are,' he added quickly. 'But unless you are, then there's no real point or need in micromanaging every single aspect of the day. Pick a general vibe, decide what matters, and let the rest go.'

'I can…do that?'

Millie waved a hand at the stack of wedding information that seemed to be breeding on her coffee table. Giles could swear there was already more there than when he'd arrived.

'These all seem to say that the perfect wedding is all in the details, and Tabby's checklist is twenty gazillion pages long, and—'

Giles reached over and put his hands on her shoulders. He was relieved that the sparks stayed away—even if his blood seemed to warm, just at being close to her. Her breath hitched, too, but he suspected that had more to do with wedding panic than his proximity.

'Breathe. Honestly. It's just a wedding—just one day. The marriage is what matters. The wedding day...? It can be anything you want. So... What matters most to you?'

'Well, the flowers, obviously. And the groom! But I've got those two things covered. After that...'

He pulled back as she bit her bottom lip, her brow furrowed as she thought. It was hard, suddenly, to remember that he'd once been so envious of this woman, whom his imagination had built up to be perfect and in control.

Suddenly Millie smiled, and it felt as if the whole room lit up.

'Cake,' she said decisively. 'I want a really incredible cake.'

Giles returned her grin and pulled out one of the invitation samples to start a new list on the back.

'Then that's where we'll start. With cake.'

* * *

Millie hadn't expected Giles to actually be any help when he arrived on her doorstep that evening, but to her surprise, by the time he left at just after midnight, they had a comprehensive list of things she cared about for the wedding, another email listing things she could delegate mostly to Tabby and her mother, and an appointment for a cake-tasting in a few weeks' time at a bakery owned by a friend of Giles's sister, who had been delighted to squeeze them in.

They'd also finished the bottle of Prosecco. But, since he was driving and had refused more than the one small glass he'd started with, Millie had to admit that was mostly her.

It was also probably why she'd hugged him as he left.

She hadn't meant to, but he'd just been so *unexpectedly* helpful and kind she hadn't been able to help herself.

It had absolutely nothing at all to do with wanting to feel his body against hers again, because she wasn't that sort of woman. Wild oats be damned.

He'd coughed awkwardly at her thanks, told her it was nothing, and then left to drive back to London—which probably meant that their next interaction would be as awkward as all the ones they'd had before Octavia's wedding.

But at least there would be cake.

And so, this Saturday lunchtime, she waited outside the shop nervously for Giles to pick her up.

It had meant leaving Holly and Ivy in the capable hands of her assistant for the afternoon, but Kayla had sworn she was up to the responsibility and—well, Millie supposed she'd have to start letting her look after things solo sooner rather than later.

Once she was married...

One thing at a time. Let's deal with the cake first.

Giles's car was, as she'd imagined it would be, sleek, high-powered and probably incredibly expensive—just like the man himself. He pulled away from the kerb before she'd even finished buckling herself in, barely managing to grunt hello.

Which was good, really. Because he looked even more damn attractive when he was glowering. But she didn't need that kind of energy in her life, so it was easier than usual to remind herself that chemistry was not what she needed in a relationship.

'Well, you're in a good mood,' she said, as they sped out of the village.

'I had a visit with my sister,' Giles replied. 'It's never good for my temperament—or my temper.'

Millie frowned. She hadn't even known he *had* a sister until he'd mentioned her friend with the bakery. 'She didn't like it that we were going to her friend's bakery for a cake?'

He glanced over briefly, frowning before returning his attention to the road. 'Why would she care about that?'

'Because you said... Never mind.'

Clearly he wasn't in a mood to talk about anything—and, really, his relationship with his sister was none of her business, anyway. The only thing they had in common right now was getting this wedding organised in Charlie's absence.

Once she'd said 'I do' to Charlie, she and Giles would probably go back to being disapproving acquaintances with nothing but Charlie in common. Which was for the best.

It was definitely for the best. Even if she wasn't sure she should be having to spend so much time reminding herself of that fact.

The rest of the drive was mostly silent, until they pulled into the village where the bakery was located—about halfway between Millie's home and Charlie's, which was convenient.

'I don't get on with her husband,' Giles said suddenly.

It took Millie a moment to cast her mind back and figure out what he was talking about.

'I should have stopped her marrying him,' he said.

'I don't think you can have that kind of sway

over anyone else's life, Giles,' Millie said, with a rueful smile. 'Not even your sister's.'

'Maybe not.' He opened the car door. 'But I still should have tried harder.'

Millie followed him, frowning. She wasn't used to any of Charlie's schoolfriends *really* taking responsibility for their actions—let alone for things that weren't even their responsibility to feel guilty over.

Maybe this was part of Charlie's plan. He'd always wanted her and Giles to be better friends—actually, to be even vaguely friendly towards each other at all. She wouldn't put it past him to have engineered a situation in which they'd have to actually get to know each other and get over all their preconceived notions about the other before the wedding. She knew well enough that after all these years Giles was as much a part of Charlie's life as she was, and she could understand him not wanting a lifetime of them sniping at each other in his future.

The bakery—called Cherry On Top, according to the swirly lettered sign—was pink and sweet and it smelled fantastic. It was also warm inside, compared to the cooling late-afternoon air. They were almost into November already, and Millie could smell the colder weather coming in the air.

'Giles!' A petite blonde woman stepped out from behind the counter, beaming as she wrapped Giles into a huge hug. 'I couldn't believe it when

Rebekah told me!' She turned to Millie. 'And you must be the fiancée! It's so exciting to meet you. We were starting to think that Giles would *never* get serious about anybody—and now here you are, choosing a cake!'

Millie's eyes widened as she looked at the woman in horror. 'Oh, no! That's not—'

'Tuppence, I'm not the groom,' Giles said calmly. 'My friend Charlie is. But he's away on business, so I'm here as part of my best man duties.'

Tuppence's face fell, and she pouted at him as she stepped back from Millie. 'I should have known it was too good to be true.'

'Yes, you should,' Giles replied with a grim smile. 'I thought you knew me better than that.'

Tuppence shrugged. 'What can I say? I'm a romantic. And when Rebekah told me you needed a wedding cake tasting session... Well, I thought that maybe you'd *finally* got over that whole "never getting married" phase.'

'It's not a phase.' Giles's response sounded like one he'd given often over the years.

'I take it this is a conversation you two have had before?' Millie observed.

It really was surprising how much she was learning about Charlie's other best friend today. And they hadn't even got to his taste in cakes yet.

She'd never really thought of Giles as a person apart from Charlie before. It was weird...

Giles rolled his eyes. 'Tuppence here has been my sister's best friend since before I was even born. She thinks that gives her the right to pass judgement on my life choices.'

'Make better choices and I won't have to,' Tuppence said, smiling widely. 'But we're not here for you and your disastrous outlook on life today. We're here for cake! So, Millie, right? Let's have a cup of tea and talk about what you're looking for, shall we?'

Tuppence led them through to a side room off the main bakery counter, where a bistro-style table was set up beside a long counter with cake stands on it, each loaded with a different sort of cake. She motioned Millie and Giles to take a seat, and moments later joined them, carrying a tray with a teapot and three cups and saucers on it, which she placed between them on the table.

'So,' she said, as the tea brewed in the pot, 'tell me about your wedding, Millie. And your groom! What sort of things do you like? Dislike? What's your theme? Your colours? That sort of thing.'

'Um…' This should be easy. She'd known Charlie almost her whole life. She knew his likes and dislikes almost as well as her own. But having to act as the *owner* or guardian of those likes and dislikes just felt…weird.

'It's a Christmas Eve wedding,' Giles put in for her. 'It'll be at Howard Hall, of course—Tabby is doing a lot of the organising—but I think Millie and Charlie are hoping to rein her in on a few things. And Millie is a florist, so she's organising the flowers. In fact, she has sketches...'

He nudged her arm, and Millie reached into her bag for the sketches she'd brought, suddenly on firmer ground. Flowers were something she could talk about.

'I thought, since it's Christmas, we'd go with the classic deep green foliage with accents of red and white—although not together, of course.'

'Of course,' Tuppence agreed, nodding sagely.

Giles, meanwhile, looked baffled. 'Why not together?'

'It's unlucky,' Millie explained. 'Supposed to symbolise death.'

'And you believe that?' He raised his eyebrows incredulously.

'No,' Millie admitted. 'But I guarantee that someone on Tabby and Lady Howard's vast invitation list will, and they're bound to mention it. Loudly. It's just easier to avoid it all together. So, white flowers for the service at the family chapel, and for the buttonholes and bouquets, but a jolly red for the table centrepieces and decorations in the reception hall.'

'Sounds perfect.' Tuppence beamed. 'And these sketches are glorious! I love the wooden bases for the centrepieces.'

Millie shrugged. 'It's probably a bit rustic for Tabby, but when she started talking about deep green being perfect for my complexion, suddenly all I could picture was a winter forest in the snow and… Well, this is where I ended up.'

'It's beautiful,' Tuppence said firmly. 'And I've got some fantastic ideas already for how we can echo this on the cake! But first…let's talk flavours.'

'And taste some, I hope,' Giles added. 'I skipped lunch.'

Tuppence laughed. 'I promise you, you will not be hungry by the time we've finished here.'

Tuppence had been right—Giles certainly wasn't hungry by the time they left the bakery. They'd tasted types of cakes that he hadn't even known existed, flavours he hadn't dreamed of—and they were all delicious. Tuppence definitely knew what she was doing.

And yet as they left—Millie having chosen something both tasteful and tasty that he was almost certain nobody could object to on the grounds of wedding superstition or anything else—he found himself craving something savoury. All that sugar had left his teeth aching and his stomach rebelling.

'I know this sounds ridiculous,' he said, as he swerved Millie away from the car, 'but I need chips. Come on, let's check out the local pub.'

'I'm so glad you said that.' Millie grinned up

at him. 'All that sugar has left me a little queasy. I need salt.'

The local pub—The Bell—was more or less exactly as Giles had expected. Scrubbed wood tables, menus clipped to tiny wooden boards, tasteful fairy lights strung around the beams and a small fir tree trimmed in gold in a pot by the door, advertising their Christmas menu.

They grabbed a table by the fire, and ordered chips at the bar.

'So. Tuppence is lovely…' Millie said, in that sort of leading way Rebekah always did when she was saying one thing but meaning another. 'She seemed disappointed about your determination not to marry, though…'

Oh, so that was it. Millie had reached her *I'm so happily loved up I want everyone else to be as happy as I am* stage. He supposed it was inevitable, but he'd hoped he might be able to avoid it for a bit longer. Not least because it was hard to imagine wanting anyone else when he was still remembering holding her body against his as they danced.

'Tuppence is very happily engaged to her girlfriend,' he said, nipping *that* idea in the bud.

'Oh.' Millie looked genuinely disappointed for a moment, before rallying as their chips arrived. 'Still, how can you be so certain you never want to get married? Maybe you just haven't—'

'Met the right person yet?' He reached for the

vinegar and doused his bowl liberally. 'Trust me—I'm sure. It's not about the person.'

She gave him an odd look as she sprinkled salt on her chips. 'I'm pretty sure that's *exactly* what marriage is about, Giles.'

They swapped condiments, and he was surprised to see she added just as much vinegar to her bowl as he had. Usually people accused him of drowning his chips. His mother said it was 'positively common'. Which might or might not have been why he started doing it; now he just liked the taste.

'Not for me.'

It wasn't something he liked to explain, but when Millie just kept looking at him, waiting as she ate her chips, he knew she wasn't going to give up without more of an explanation.

'I just… Marriage isn't something that goes well in my family. And I have no reason to believe that I'd be any better at it. So I think it's better for everyone if I just…don't.'

'You said you don't get on with your sister's husband,' she said, eyeing him carefully. 'What about your parents?'

'I don't really get on with either of them, either.' He said it half as a joke, even though it was perfectly truthful.

She didn't laugh.

'I *meant* how do they feel about you swearing off marriage? I mean, Charlie's parents have been on at him about marrying and continuing the family name, providing heirs and that sort of thing for *years*, now.' She stopped suddenly, her cheeks pink in the firelight. 'Not that that's why he's marrying *me*, or anything.'

Giles laughed. 'I never thought it was. If that was the case, he'd have done it years ago.'

The idea that Charlie might only be marrying Millie to keep his parents happy was absurd. He watched as she smiled shyly at him and thought that he could list five or six reasons to marry Millie right off the top of his head, if he had to.

For *Charlie* to marry her, anyway. Obviously. Marriage wasn't what he thought about when he looked at Millie. That was definitely something less…respectable.

But Charlie had merely come around to seeing what was right in front of him all along—like in all those Christmas romcoms Rebekah liked to pretend she didn't watch, but blubbed at every time.

Truly, it was the time of year for miracles, and all that. Or it would be by the time the wedding rolled around.

'And in answer to your question… I have both a niece and a nephew. What is left of our family estate can carry on perfectly well without me when I'm gone.'

Not the name, though; Rebekah had taken her husband's name when she married, and the children had his name, too. Something else he didn't deserve, but that was the way of the world.

What his brother-in-law *did* have, though, was money. As did Giles. His niece and nephew would never have to worry about making ends meet—and that would be far easier for them if he got rid of the money pit of the house first.

Millie gave him a curious look. 'What's left of your family estate? Is it crumbling into the sea or something?'

'It might as well be.' He reached for another chip—hot and salty and tangy with vinegar—and focussed on the taste in his mouth to distract him from the feelings that the subject made swirl around his chest. 'The house is falling apart, the land is poorly maintained, and my parents won't do anything to change that.'

'Oh. I'm sorry. I didn't… I didn't realise.'

There was a confused frown between her eyebrows, as if she were readjusting her view of the world in light of this new information.

He gave her what he hoped was a reassuring smile. 'No reason why you should.'

He hadn't intended to get into a discussion of his family's net worth, but if they were going to be spending time together planning her wedding, he supposed it was inevitable that they get to know each other better than they'd ever bothered to in the past.

'Fortunately, my personal wealth is intact. It's only the estate that's going to the dogs.'

The little frown line deepened. Giles was horrified to discover he found it *cute*.

'That's why I… I mean, Charlie always says that you're richer than any of them these days. So why don't you—?' She broke off. 'I'm sorry. It's none of my business.'

She was right; it wasn't her business. And normally Giles would take the way out—change the subject to something less likely to make him want to drink. But for some reason he didn't want her to think worse of him than she always had. Because things were different now from back when they'd both been competing for Charlie's friendship and happily loathing each other behind his back.

God help him, he wanted Charlie's bride to *like* him. Because if she didn't she'd have the power to cut him out of his best friend's life, and he wasn't sure he could take that.

Charlie was the only thing that had made boarding school—even university—bearable. He didn't want to lose that friendship. Even if it meant telling Millie the truths he usually tried to keep close to his chest.

'You don't understand why I don't just bail out my parents and pay for the estate repairs and so on?' He gave a wry smile. 'Neither do they.'

'But you have a reason.' Millie gazed at him

steadily. 'And I'd wager it's a good one. You don't have to explain it to me.'

He blinked in surprise. Whatever he'd expected from her, it wasn't this blind and trusting acceptance. More likely, he'd have predicted suspicion and scepticism.

He wondered if this was what Charlie saw in her eyes every time she smiled at him. If so, he couldn't believe it had taken his friend this long to propose.

'I didn't expect you to have such faith in me,' he said carefully. 'I'm almost certain you never used to.'

Millie gave a small shrug and reached for another chip. 'That was years ago. I figure if Charlie has kept you around all this time, he must see something in you I didn't. Besides...'

She bit her lip, and Giles found he couldn't look away from where her white teeth pressed against the pink flesh.

'Besides?'

'You're here,' she said, looking down at the table. 'I know Charlie would be here, doing all this, if he could, but since he's had to go away... you've really stepped up to help me, and I appreciate that. You could have easily just called and asked if I needed anything, then accepted my answer when I said I was fine. But you didn't. And... Well, that tells me a lot about you that I didn't know before.'

Suddenly a hot anger filled his chest—with himself, for hating this woman for so long, but mostly with Charlie, for leaving her when she needed him. For forcing her to make do with Giles instead—a man so unsuited for the task that it had to be seen to be believed.

Charlie should be here, not him. If only because when Millie looked up with those sparkling, hopeful eyes, her lips slightly parted, Charlie could kiss her and Giles couldn't.

Not that he wanted to. Okay, fine. He wanted to. He'd wanted to do a lot more than kiss her since Octavia's wedding. But he *wouldn't*—and that was what mattered. Wasn't it?

Surely this ridiculous attraction would pass soon. Before the wedding, ideally.

But what if it *didn't*?

At first, he'd assumed his sudden passion had been brought about by her looking gorgeous at the wedding, and weddings being the sort of occasion when he usually pulled women. After that, maybe he'd felt a bit of a 'one that got away' thing for her. And then he guessed he'd just been feeling sorry for her after Charlie absconded.

But what if it was more than that?

What if he spent the rest of his life wishing he could kiss Millie Myles? Not because she looked good in a dress, or because he couldn't have her, but because of the woman she was.

Because of how he felt about her.

Oh, hell.

'Anyway, since you *are* here...'

Oblivious to the internal confusion that had set Giles's world in a spin, Millie smiled and carried on talking.

'I promised Tabby and Charlie's mother that I'd head up to Howard Hall the weekend after next to finalise some arrangements for the venue. Do you think you could come with me? Help me stand my ground so I don't end up with gold-encrusted beef for the wedding breakfast, or something.'

He laughed, despite himself. 'I don't think Tabby would waste gold on the guests. More likely she'll have found some crown or other for you to wear with the antique family veil.'

Millie groaned. 'Oh, God, the dress... That's a whole different argument I need to have with them. They don't seem to realise that there isn't a chance of me fitting into any of their family heirloom gowns. I'm hoping I can just get away with ordering one from some website in China...'

The idea of Millie in a wedding gown—antique or otherwise—seemed about ready to short-circuit his brain. He hoped to God she had other people to take her dress shopping—he was fairly sure Tabby wouldn't let *that* responsibility get delegated to him.

But Millie was waiting for an answer.

In light of what he'd just realised—quite how much he wanted to kiss his best friend's fiancée, and not just to get her into bed, but just *because*—he knew he should say no. He was busy…had work commitments he couldn't get out of just like Charlie. She'd buy it and never know the difference.

And yet when he opened his mouth to reply, the words that came out were, 'Sure. I'll pick you up on my way.'

CHAPTER SEVEN

GILES WAS QUIET on their drive up to Howard Hall, a couple of weeks later. Millie had hoped to talk about the things she needed to stay firm on, but all attempts at conversation had been met with non-conversational grunts or hums.

'Late night last night?' she asked eventually.

She'd never seen Giles hungover, but she assumed this was what it looked like.

He gave her a wan smile. 'No. Just a long week. At work.'

'Right.'

She had no reason to disbelieve him, but she couldn't shake the feeling he wasn't telling her something. Instead of pressing him further, she shifted in her seat and stared out of her window at the passing countryside instead.

She hadn't pressed him on his family the other night in the pub, either. Maybe she should have, because curiosity had been eating her up ever since. In the moment it had seemed more important to show him that she trusted him—or at least was beginning to trust him, as Charlie's other oldest friend—than to get all the gossip. But Millie had to admit she did have a bit of a weakness for… Not gossip. *Understanding* people.

She wanted to *understand* Giles. As a… Well, as a friend, she supposed.

As an outsider in Charlie's world, she knew there were myriad things she'd never understand about the life high-society people lived, even if she was expected to join it. She'd never been to boarding school, or to Oxford. Nor even skiing, as it happened.

In the same way that Charlie would never understand about having to budget down to the penny for the weekly food shop, or knowing that a bad month at the shop could be the difference between paying her rent or not, she'd never fully understand his upbringing—or Giles's either.

But she wanted to at least try.

Maybe if she knew him better as a person she'd move past the ridiculous crush that had had her blushing when he opened the car door for her, or when his hand brushed hers over a bowl of chips.

She'd given in to her curiosity on a video call with Charlie earlier in the week. Once they'd got through the wedding update, she'd mentioned her conversation with Giles about his family.

'What *is* the deal with him and his parents?' she'd asked, trying to sound casual.

Charlie had raised his eyebrows. 'Since when do you care about Giles Fairfax's life?'

'Since you left him to be my wedding planner,' she'd replied pointedly.

But Charlie hadn't caved. 'It's not my story to tell.'

So Giles remained as much of a mystery to her as ever. Aloof and secretive, and today silent and grumpy. But he was still here and, quite aside from the fact that looking at his handsome profile was always fun, she was grateful for the company.

Doubly glad, in fact, once they reached Howard Hall.

Tabby and Lady Howard were surprised to see Giles accompanying her, that much was clear on their arrival, but they took it in their stride, like everything else.

Millie wasn't sure if that was an aristocratic thing, or a trait bred from running events at their many properties, but either way it worked for her. Giles had merely explained that Charlie had asked him to stand in for some things while he was away, and everyone had nodded, as if that was a perfectly normal thing for a best man to do.

But he proved she'd been right to ask him to come within the first twenty minutes.

As they all sat down in the front parlour, with tea and cakes, Tabby pulled out a clipboard with a familiar-looking list on it and said, 'So, Millie, have you had a chance to look at the guest list I sent over? How many names do you think you're going to want to add?'

'Um...'

They hadn't even talked about money, she realised. Charlie had told her right at the start not to worry about it—that he'd cover everything, or his family would—but Millie knew that by normal social convention it should be her family paying. She knew her mum would feel awkward about not being able to do that. Hell, she felt awkward about not paying for it herself in this day and age. Why should they be relying on their parents to fund it anyway?

Except that she'd put everything she had saved into the shop, and Charlie's career *was* the family business, so...

'I... I still need to check with Charlie about exactly who he wants to invite—you know how busy he's been up in Scotland.'

In truth, she had no idea how busy Charlie had been, or what he'd been doing, because all their conversations had been about the wedding rather than anything else in their lives. But it worked as an excuse now, because she hadn't known how to raise the question of the guest list with him. The one time she'd mentioned it, he'd just said that his mother and Tabby would know who to invite.

And, since that was sort of the problem, it hadn't really helped at all.

She glanced sideways at Giles, who appeared to be concentrating all his attention on a small iced cake.

'I do know that we were thinking that…with it being Christmas Eve and all, and people wanting to spend time with their families…maybe it would be best to keep the guest list…well, small?'

That sounded okay, didn't it? It was concern for others that was making her say that, rather than not wanting a couple of hundred of the Howards' random society acquaintances sharing the most important day of her life.

'We thought exactly the same,' Tabby said, leaning forward with a smile. 'That's why we pared down the list before we sent it to you!'

'Two hundred is "pared down"?' The words blurted out of her before she could stop them.

Tabby and her mother shared a knowing smile.

'Millie, darling, I know this is a lot for you,' Lady Howard said. 'But a wedding in our family—and in our home—is bigger than perhaps the events you're used to. To *not* invite certain people would be a serious faux pas.'

'But, as you say, maybe some of them will be busy on Christmas Eve,' Tabby added. But she didn't sound as if she believed it.

Millie shot a hopeless look at Giles. 'I just think… Charlie and I were planning something… small. Intimate. Personal.'

'It will be personal!' Tabby assured her, happily ignoring the other attributes Millie had been hoping for. 'I've got so many ideas for how we can make the whole thing really *feel* like the love you and Charlie share. Look!'

She pulled out another folder, this one filled with samples and colours and vision boards, and Millie felt the whole room go a little swimmy around her.

She couldn't do this. She couldn't marry into this family—into their expectations and their society. Except if she wanted the family she'd always dreamed of, and to give that family to her best friend, too, she had to.

She'd be happy married to Charlie—she knew that. She just had to survive the wedding planning first.

'Back to the guest list for a moment,' Giles said, and all three women looked at him in surprise.

It was the first time he'd commented on anything wedding-related since they'd arrived. Millie suspected that Tabby and Lady Howard had assumed he was only there under duress, and mostly for the food and to play chauffeur.

Millie hadn't been sure herself.

But now he seemed completely engaged in the conversation.

'I think Millie's right. Charlie really wants it to be an exclusive gathering. No photos sold to the press or a social media frenzy. I know you want to show off the venue, of course, but I think showcasing it as a truly private, exclusive wedding location would be even more effective. Not to mention it adds a certain cachet to the whole occasion.' He sat back in his chair. 'Obviously there'll be some people who need to be there, and some you'll want there. But if you keep the list small those people will feel truly special and appreciated, too. Keep if really...refined.'

This time the look that Tabby shared with her mother was more speculative. Considering, even.

Millie felt something akin to hope start to rise inside her chest and sent Giles a grateful smile. He looked away.

'A smaller guest list would mean we could do something truly ambitious with the menu,' Tabby said thoughtfully. 'Maybe even a full festive tasting menu with wine pairings.'

'And we could use more of the rooms before and after the service,' Lady Howard added. 'Yes, it *could* work.'

'Let me go and speak with Chef.' Tabby jumped up from her chair. 'He's preparing food for us to taste already, but he should also have supplies for the tasting menu on hand, for the trial run of next weekend's event, so it shouldn't be difficult to set it up. You two carry on here.'

And then she was gone, leaving Millie alone with her future mother-in-law.

No, not alone. Giles was still there.

But she wasn't sure how much there was that he could do when Lady Howard fixed her with a steely look and said, 'Now, Millie. Let's talk gowns and rings while we're waiting.'

Giles had done his best on the guest list thing, but he knew when he was beaten. Lady Howard's expression told him that she and Millie would be discussing wedding dresses and rings with or without him—and without him sounded definitely preferable.

He shot Millie an apologetic look as he slipped out of the room, phone in hand, as if it had silently buzzed with an incoming call. From the betrayed look on Millie's face, she knew it hadn't.

Outside, the air was turning wintry already—cold and grey, with a slight haze hanging over the fields. Giles leaned against the ancient stone of Howard Hall and swiped across his phone to place a call.

'How's it going?' Charlie asked, the minute he answered.

'I think we've managed to persuade your mother and sister to keep the guest list under a thousand or so. But you may now have a twelve-course tasting menu wedding breakfast as a result.'

Charlie groaned. 'Is Millie okay?'

'Your mother is currently talking to her about wedding gowns and heirloom rings.'

No point sugar-coating it. He imagined Millie would be calling her fiancé later to share the misery anyway. Might as well give his friend a heads-up for what was in store.

'I should be there.' Guilt sounded heavy in Charlie's voice.

'Trust me, I would definitely rather you were here than me,' Giles said. 'And I'm sure Millie would, too.' He paused, wondering whether to add the next bit. Then he decided that he and Charlie hadn't stayed best friends for so long by not saying what needed to be said. 'Why aren't you?'

'This movie…up here in Scotland. I need to be here. For the…antiques…insurance purposes. You know?'

'Right. Insurance.'

It wasn't that Giles thought Charlie was lying. It was just… Surely he could have got away for a day or two, to do this with Millie?

And it wasn't that Giles minded standing in. If he was honest with himself, he was enjoying it all a lot more than he'd imagined he would— and he knew a lot of that came from just getting to spend time with Millie. But he hated seeing her so lost without Charlie there.

He knew he could never really be a replacement for their mutual best friend.

'Tell Millie I'm really sorry she's having to do this alone,' said Charlie. Then there was a commotion on the other end of the line. 'Sorry, I'm going to have to go.'

The line went dead, just as he heard Charlie shouting 'Liberty!' as he walked away.

Yeah, maybe Charlie would rather be here than in Scotland. But it didn't change the fact that he wasn't.

With a sigh, Giles turned and headed back inside—only to crash into Tabby in the hall.

'*There* you are. Come on! We're menu-tasting. Chef is cooking *everything*. I hope you're hungry!'

His stomach growled in response. 'Apparently so. Lead on!'

At least there were *some* good things about his additional best man duties.

Even if it meant helping Millie get married to their mutual best friend and ignoring the guilt he felt about imagining what they could be doing if she *wasn't* marrying another man...

Four hours later, Millie was so full she didn't think she could stand. 'You're going to have to roll me out to the car,' she told Giles, after they'd made their goodbyes to Tabby and Lady Howard. 'I don't think I can see my feet any more.'

The food had been delicious—all of it—and there would have been no way Millie could have decided between all the fantastic options alone. Luckily, the other three diners had had plenty of opinions, so mostly Millie's job had been to agree with them. By the end of the tasting session they'd had a menu of seven small courses that would apparently be perfect for the Christmas Eve wedding.

'I thought your mother was the cook at Howard Hall.' Giles opened the car door for her. 'The man cooking today didn't look a thing like you.'

She rolled her eyes as she collapsed into the passenger seat. 'Mum is the *family* cook. They have a whole kitchen and a pseudo celebrity chef for events. And besides, Mum's mostly retired these days anyway.'

She felt a pang of guilt as she looked down the long driveway in the direction of the small gatehouse where she'd grown up—and where her mother still lived.

She should have invited Mum to the tasting today. Wasn't that what parents of the bride were supposed to do? It was only that, as much as the Howards had always made them feel a part of the family…they weren't. They were staff. And she knew her mother felt that.

Yes, Jessica Myles had been excited, supportive—delighted, even, when they'd announced the engagement. But as they'd sipped sherry with the Howards that day she'd watched as her mum grew silent, fading into the background as Charlie's family took over with their wedding plans and expectations.

Millie and her mother couldn't contribute financially to the wedding. She didn't even have a father to give her away—although she'd already told Charlie *and* Tabby, in no uncertain terms, that her mother would be doing that, and neither of them had dared to argue with her about it.

But now the wedding plans were continuing apace, and she hadn't even thought to invite her mum.

As Giles pulled away from Howard Hall and started down the driveway he glanced over at her. 'Do you want to stop and see your mum before we head back?'

She jerked her head round to stare at him in shock. 'How did you know I was thinking about her?'

He shrugged. 'You're kind of an open book, you know. Easy to read.'

Except she wasn't. Because if she was he'd already know that this wedding wasn't quite the love match she'd been telling everyone it was.

And *that* was the real reason she'd been avoiding her mum. She knew Millie better than anyone—better, even, than Charlie. If anyone was going to guess, it was Jessica Myles.

But, oh, she wanted her mum to believe that her little girl was marrying for true love. That this really was the fairytale ending everyone kept saying it was.

She swallowed. She'd just have to be a better actress, then, wouldn't she?

'Yeah, if you don't mind. I'd like to stop in if we have time.'

'At your service, milady,' Giles said, and pulled over at the gatehouse.

Her mum was surprised to see them—that much was clear.

'Millie! I didn't know you were visiting. Is Charlie home, then?'

Her gaze darted towards Giles, then back to Millie, looking for an answer to the unspoken question of what she was doing there with her fiancé's best man.

'No, he's still in Scotland.'

Millie stripped off her winter coat and hung it on one of the hooks by the door, just as she'd done every day throughout her childhood. In fact, under the normal-height hooks were a series of brightly coloured plastic ones at varying heights, which her father had put up for her to use as she grew. Neither she nor her mum had ever had the heart to take them down.

'I had to come and meet with Tabby and Lady Howard about some arrangements and the menu. Giles agreed to come and help me avoid being steamrollered.'

'And how did that go?'

Her mum raised an eyebrow as Millie unwound her scarf and moved out of the way for Giles to add his own smart, tailored wool coat to the hooks.

'Is it still your wedding or is it Tabby's now?'

Millie laughed. 'Still mine—just about. They had this ridiculous guest list, but Giles persuaded them to tone it down.'

'In exchange for an equally excessive tasting menu,' Giles added. 'But I've always preferred food to people, so that works for me.'

Millie's mum laughed at that. She realised her mother had probably never spent any time with Giles before—even Millie hadn't really, so why would her mum? But she already had her arm through his, leading him through to the little sitting room and promising to put the kettle on in a moment since, even if they *were* still full from the tasting, there was always room for tea.

She felt a pang in her chest as she watched them go, both joking and laughing. It should be Charlie here with her and her mum—her actual fiancé joking about wedding plans. Not the stand-in Charlie had sent because she needed back-up.

Not for the first time since she and Charlie had cooked up their plan, a wave of uncertainty rushed through her. Was she crazy to be doing this? Did the fact that Charlie was to be hundreds of miles away for basically their entire engagement mean he was getting cold feet? He swore not, whenever they spoke on the phone, and she'd always been able to tell when he was lying before. But still the doubt lingered.

And she had to admit spending time with Giles wasn't helping with that. Oh, it wasn't that she imagined for a moment she could have the kind of future she wanted with Giles, but that was her mind talking. Her body definitely had other ideas.

Lucky that she'd learnt that passion wasn't to be trusted, really.

I can trust Giles, though.

The thought caught her by surprise—mostly because she realised it was true. Somehow her childhood enemy had become the one person she trusted to help her navigate her way through this whole wedding chaos. She *almost* wished she could tell him the truth.

In the lounge, she swept her fingers over a delicate, crocheted blanket in shades of grey and white that her mother had hung over the back of one of the upright dining chairs at the tiny table in the bay window. It was unfinished, obviously a work in progress, and just as obviously intended for a baby.

'Mrs Pratchett in the village…her daughter is expecting. Doesn't want to find out the sex—or isn't telling if she has—and she's gone for an all-neutral nursery, which seems to mean grey and white.' Her mum looked with dissatisfaction at the blanket. 'Not the colours I would have chosen for a baby—you want joyous colours for that, and grey always feels a bit depressing, don't you think? But grey's what they want, so grey is what they're getting—it's their baby, after all, not mine. And I think it'll be pretty enough when it's finished.'

'It's beautiful.'

The words choked her; she could feel her eyes pricking and her throat swelling. Oh, God, she really couldn't cry over a baby blanket. Then her mum would definitely know something was wrong—and the last thing she wanted to do was tell her about her fertility issues and have her guessing the real reason she was marrying Charlie. She'd be so disappointed in her, for not holding out for the sort of true love she and Millie's dad had once had.

But Jessica Myles only smiled and squeezed her shoulder. 'Maybe I'll be making one for you and Charlie before too long. Not grey, though,' she added, as a warning.

Millie laughed, and was pleased it didn't come out too soggy. 'Definitely not grey, Mum. I promise.'

'Good.' One last squeeze of the shoulder, and she moved away towards the kitchen. 'Come on. I've set Giles to laying the tea tray. Let's see how he's got on.'

It was several hours later—after many cups of tea and even a round or two of cheese on toast, when the effects of the tasting menu wore off—before Millie and Giles left the gatehouse.

'Safe travels home,' Jessica told Giles, as he went to warm up the car.

He gave her a mock salute in return, before disappearing into the darkness and leaving Millie alone with her mum.

'He's not like the rest of Charlie's old schoolfriends, is he?' Jessica mused. 'I remember the state they used to leave the house in when his parents went away and they'd have a party. Maybe he was the same as the rest of them back then, but he at least seems to have grown up—which is more than you can say for some of them.' She gave a satisfied nod. 'Charlie chose well for his best man. I'm glad he's here to help you out while Charlie's away.'

'Me too,' Millie replied, surprised to realise how much she meant it. 'He's been great, actually. And I wasn't expecting that.'

If anything, she'd expected Giles to treat her as a burden, or as if he was doing her a massive favour—which he was—and to expect constant gratitude in return. Instead, he'd just been there, quietly doing exactly what she needed even when she wasn't sure quite what that was. Like coming to visit her mum. He'd known that was what she needed even before she had.

But there were some wedding-related things

he simply couldn't do. Or at least things that she wouldn't feel comfortable asking him to do.

'Mum, are you free to go down to London one day in the next couple of weeks?' Millie asked.

'I can be,' Jessica replied. 'What for?'

'Well, if I'm not going to try to squeeze into one of the Howard wedding gowns…we're going to need to go dress shopping.'

CHAPTER EIGHT

LONDON WAS READY for Christmas. Never mind
that it was only November, the city wasn't waiting. The lights were up and sparkling, the air
smelled of roasting chestnuts and hot chocolate,
people in shops were wearing Santa hats, and the
whole city was absolutely rammed with people.

Giles hated London at this time of year.

Normally, he'd do everything he could to avoid
having to come into the centre of London during
November or December. His offices in the City
weren't nearly so bad.

But Charlie hadn't made it home for his appointment at the jewellers to choose a ring. So
here he was, getting ready to meet Millie again
and play the part of stand-in groom once more.

It was getting to be a problem, he admitted to
himself as he sipped a coffee at the window bar of
an overheated and overcrowded coffee shop near
where she'd asked to meet him. Just as well that
in a month or so Charlie would be back, they'd

get married, and he could get on with his life away from them.

Okay, not totally away. Charlie was still his best friend, and Millie was certainly becoming something. But he wouldn't have to be in their pockets the whole time, at their beck and call, with their wedding the most important thing in his life.

If he wanted, he could stay away for weeks on end.

Except then he wouldn't see Millie. And the idea of that...

Well, this was why it was becoming a problem.

He *liked* his best friend's fiancée.

Liked as in it was getting harder and harder to imagine never kissing her. Not seeing her, talking to her regularly. Not being the person she turned to for things.

And that was *definitely* a problem.

Chemistry and attraction was one thing—he could handle that. What he wasn't used to was just wanting to be near another person this way. Thank God she *was* marrying someone else, or he might actually have to stop and examine what the feeling meant, and that couldn't end well.

It didn't matter, anyway. He couldn't do anything about it—wouldn't even let on about his feelings if he could help it, because that wouldn't be fair to anyone. Millie was engaged to Charlie, and he didn't want to do anything that could possibly disrupt that.

Not least because they were such a perfect fit. They both wanted the same things—marriage, family, the fairytale. Things that Giles categorically did *not* want. So it would be utterly unfair for him to say anything and add even the smallest smidgen of uncertainty into the proceedings.

If he were a humbler man, he'd doubt that anything he said or did could possibly shake the love Charlie and Millie shared. And long term he was sure that was true. But right now...in the moment...

Millie was anxious about the wedding—that much was obvious—and Charlie being away wasn't helping her confidence either. More than that...sometimes she looked at him, too. Oh, she looked away again, fast, but he still saw it—hoped for it, even. Those brief moments when he caught her considering as she watched him. Wondering, maybe, what it would be like to kiss him—the same way *he* wondered about her.

He shook his head and took another sip of coffee. It was pointless dwelling on it. Millie was marrying Charlie and nothing was going to change that—he wouldn't let it. She was just having pre-wedding jitters, and he wasn't going to be the bastard who took advantage of that.

So, instead, he drained the rest of his coffee and got to his feet, escaping the roasting coffee shop for the crisp, cool November air outside. Millie had been shopping with her mother that morning, and had asked him to meet her at their last shop and go on to the jewellers, which was nearby.

Apparently, Charlie had sent in an order for their wedding rings, but he wanted Millie to choose her own engagement ring. Which made sense—apart from the bit where *Giles* was the one shopping for it with her.

Still, once they left the shop he'd keep hold of the wedding rings, in his capacity as best man, and she'd be wearing the engagement ring. Maybe a huge freaking diamond on her left hand would help him get it through his thick head that she was not for him.

He could only hope.

Except the shop where Millie had asked him to meet her was a wedding dress boutique. And she was running late.

Giles pushed open the door and stepped inside to see Millie draped in ivory satin, looking like a goddess in an off-the-shoulder gown. And any words he might have intended to say to announce his arrival disappeared.

'Giles!'

She looked flustered at his arrival—maybe even as flustered as he felt seeing her in a wedding gown—for all that she'd asked him to come.

'Now, now… It's bad luck for the groom to see the bride in her dress before the wedding day!'

The boutique owner approached him with an incongruous fan in her hand—one he suspected she was about to hit him with, before Jessica laughed and said, 'Oh, that's not the groom. It's the best man.'

Millie, bright red, had bustled away behind some screens to a changing area, but her voice carried back into the room.

'Besides, I'm not sure that's the dress. I like it, but…' She trailed off.

'You looked amazing in it,' Giles said—hopefully helpfully. 'But I didn't see the others.'

'They all looked beautiful,' Jessica said loyally. 'But that last one was something special.'

Too damn right it was.

'I'm just not sure…'

Millie emerged from behind the screened-off area of the changing rooms, this time dressed in her more usual jeans and a warm, snowflake-patterned jumper. Giles cursed inwardly as he realised he still wanted to strip that woollen layer off her every bit as much as he had the ivory gown.

'Well, there aren't very many dress shops that can get you *any* wedding dress ready and perfectly fitted before Christmas Eve,' the boutique owner said. 'If it weren't for the fact that Tabitha asked me personally... Anyway... I wouldn't leave it too late.'

'I won't,' Millie promised. 'I'll go through the photos Mum took and make a decision tonight, then I'll be in touch tomorrow. Thank you so much for your help.'

They said their goodbyes to Jessica, who assured them she would be fine catching the train back after 'a bit of a mooch around the shops' on the lookout for Christmas presents.

Giles personally couldn't think of anything worse.

Or at least he thought he couldn't. Until they reached the jeweller's shop.

Collecting the rings Charlie had ordered was an easy enough job. The owner—who had been supplying fine jewellery to the Howard family for decades, possibly centuries—checked his ID against the name and details Charlie had supplied, nodded, and went to retrieve the bands from a safe, leaving his assistant to keep a beady eye on Giles and Millie as they perused engagement rings.

'They're all so *expensive*,' Millie whispered to him as she stared at the trays of sparkling diamonds.

The assistant took a step closer, apparently not reassured that they belonged in such a fine establishment. Giles expected it had something to do with the fluffy snowflakes on Millie's jumper, which he was trying very hard not to find adorable.

'Do you have any idea what sort of thing you're looking for?' he asked.

Millie's eyes only widened.

'Well, did you and Charlie discuss a style? Or even a budget?'

'Not really,' Millie admitted.

Giles was beginning to wonder if the pair of them had discussed *anything* about this wedding before Charlie hightailed it to Scotland.

'He just said that he wanted me to choose something that felt like *me*, no matter what it cost.'

She gave a sheepish but besotted smile, and Giles felt his jaw tense.

'He knew I didn't like the idea of wearing one of the family rings, beautiful as they are. They're too fancy for me—and totally impractical for my work.'

He hadn't considered how rings might impact her floristry career. He supposed having huge, valuable gems that could get caught on delicate petals or, worse, lost in buckets of water, was not a great idea.

'Okay, let's start over here, then,' he suggested, pointing at a display of more modern rings, many with lower profile settings.

He stood back, hands in his pockets, as she considered the offerings. But then one ring caught his eye, and he just knew it would be perfect.

'What about this one?'

The words were out before he could stop himself—something that seemed to be becoming a problem around her. But the way her eyes lit up when she saw the ring he was suggesting made it all worthwhile.

'Oh, wow, that's *perfect*,' she breathed.

It was gold, which would match the wedding bands Charlie had ordered, but instead of the usual diamond a bright green emerald sat in the wide band. The band itself had two tiny rubies inset on either side. The emerald matched her eyes, Giles thought, not to mention the greenery she worked with every day. And the rubies made him think of the holly she'd insisted had to feature in her bouquet.

Giles motioned to the shop assistant and got him to open the case, then plucked the ring from its cushioned case. 'Hold out your hand.'

'It'll probably need resizing,' Millie told him, even as she gave him her hand. 'I have chubby fingers. But still— Oh!'

She broke off as he slid the ring onto the third finger of her left hand. It fitted perfectly, nestled in position as if it had always been there.

As if he had always been the person who was fated to put it there.

Not my fiancée. I don't want *a fiancée,* he reminded himself fiercely in his head.

It didn't help. Something hot and possessive

and primal was coursing through his body, and the only thing that was stopping him from kissing her was the memory of his best friend, at one time his *only* friend, and the knowledge that he could never, ever betray Charlie.

However much his body begged him to.

He couldn't do that to Charlie.

And he couldn't make Millie promises he couldn't keep.

Giles looked up to her face and in the same movement she looked away from the ring and met his gaze. 'This is the one?' he whispered.

She swallowed, then nodded.

Giles turned back to the shop owner, who had returned with the wedding bands from the safe and was beaming at them, as if overcome by the romance of it all.

He wondered if the shopkeeper realised that he wasn't the groom.

'We'll take it.'

Giles pulled out his credit card. Charlie had told him to use his line of credit at the shop, but that would only hold things up. At least that was the excuse he made to himself for insisting on paying for the ring personally.

'Now.'

He had to get out of there—fast. Even if it meant seeing that ring on Millie's hand for the rest of the day.

* * *

Millie had a problem. And she was starting to think that she wasn't the only one suffering from it.

There was no good reason for Giles to drive her home after ring-shopping; she was perfectly capable of taking the train. But when he'd offered, she'd accepted. And when they'd arrived it had only seemed polite to invite him in—even if that meant he was now helping her stuff invitations into envelopes while the remains of their takeaway curry sat on her kitchen counter.

There was also no good explanation for the way her heart had seemed to thump twice as hard as she'd watched Giles slide her engagement ring onto her left hand. The ring that he'd spotted and chosen as the perfect ring for her. The exact ring she would have chosen for herself if she'd seen it first.

The ring she still wore now, symbolising her intention to marry another man.

There was no reason for her to feel suddenly wobbly about that decision. She'd spent so much of the past month imagining her future life with Charlie—a contented, comfortable existence with a man she loved, not in the passionate way that faded with time, but in the sort of way that lasted for ever. *That* was what she wanted. So there really was no reason to feel wobbly. At all.

But sitting there in the candlelight with Giles, sticking stamps on wedding invitations, she did.

And she'd think she was alone in that feeling except for five things.

Exhibit A: The look on his face when he'd seen her in a wedding dress.
Exhibit B: The aforementioned way he'd chosen her dream engagement ring.
Exhibit C: The fact he'd *paid* for it himself.
Exhibit D: How both driving her home and getting a takeaway had been his idea.
Exhibit E: The fact he was willingly stuffing envelopes with her instead of…whatever he usually did with his evenings in London.

Probably something involving svelte, rich society blondes and cocktails she didn't even know the names of.

This wasn't usual behaviour for any of Charlie's friends. Even taking into account that Charlie had asked him to help her out, surely this had to be above and beyond?

In her past encounters with Charlie's friends, the most any of them had wanted from her was a quick grope at a party or a one-night stand after the pub. They'd certainly never wanted to be *friends* with the likes of her. Charlie didn't know, but she'd heard more than one of them mocking him for being friends with 'the help'—never mind that she'd never actually worked at Howard Hall. She wasn't their type, and that much was obvious in every look they gave her and every word they spoke to her.

'Good enough to bed, but not good enough to wed.'

That was what her mother had said—a warning when Millie had first been invited to one of Charlie's parties up at the hall.

'You watch yourself around them boys. Stay close to Charlie. He's different. He'll look after you.'

And he had. He still was. He was marrying her, for heaven's sake.

And she was repaying him by lusting after his best friend.

Because that was what it was, of course. Just lust. She'd developed a stupid crush on Giles Fairfax when they'd danced together at Octavia's wedding and now it just wouldn't quit. But it had to eventually, didn't it? It was just chemistry, just passion, not anything real.

It was only based on the way he looked at her, the way he anticipated her needs, the way he wasn't at all the man she'd expected him to be—and probably something to do with the way he raised his eyebrows at her and smiled.

Or the way she couldn't close her eyes without imagining his hands on her waist, sweeping up over her body even as his lips worked their way down…

She opened her eyes again. Quickly. Before Giles noticed she was fantasising about him even as he sat right opposite her. She *really* didn't want him figuring that out. Because a crush was all it was—all it could be. Even if she *wasn't* engaged to Charlie, Giles wasn't interested in the kind of future that she wanted. So what was the point of even considering it? Not that she *was* considering it, of course. But if she had been it would be pointless, that was all.

She didn't want a future filled with uncertainty, always waiting for the other shoe to drop when her husband grew bored of her, when the passion faded. She wanted the certainty of a solid marriage based on friendship. With Charlie.

She just wished she didn't feel as if she was trying to convince herself of that all of a sudden.

Millie reached out for the next envelope in a rushed, jerking movement—and realised too late that Giles was doing the same. Her fingers brushed against the back of his hand, and she heard him take a sharp breath before yanking his hand away.

'Sorry. Bride first.'

God, even his voice sounded affected by her touch—suddenly lower, more gravelly than usual. As she imagined it might sound in bed.

Not that she'd imagined that.

At all.

Much.

Millie shoved the next invitation into the relevant envelope and hoped that whoever the recipient was didn't mind theirs being a little crumpled. Hopefully they'd blame it on the Royal Mail.

This was ridiculous. And none of it would be happening if Charlie was here.

She blinked, her brain stalling on the thought. *Did Charlie know this would happen?*

'Millie?'

From the way Giles said her name, she thought it wasn't the first time he'd spoken.

'You okay?'

'Yes. Of course.' She dropped the invitation and jumped to her feet. 'I was just going to make…tea. Decaf tea. Because it's late. Do you want one?'

'Sure,' Giles said, with a shrug.

But she felt his eyes on her as she walked away to hide in the kitchen, and when she glanced back there was a frown line between his eyebrows.

He knew something was up. Which was fair—because it was mostly his fault.

Except it was *Charlie's* words, or the memory of them, that had sent her world spinning.

'I meant what I said about fidelity, but we're not actually married yet. So, look, what happens in Vegas stays in Vegas. I'm fine with that. I mean, if you want a final fling or two, or what-

ever, before you say I do, *then you should go for it. Sow those wild oats, as my grandfather used to say.'*

At the time, she'd almost dismissed the idea completely—rolled her eyes and told him to go to a strip club, or whatever, for his stag and get it all out of his system. She trusted Charlie—once they were married he'd be faithful, and before then he'd be careful. She hadn't really considered that his theory might apply to her, too. After all, she'd gone plenty long enough without sex since Tom—and, really, it wasn't as if Charlie wasn't objectively gorgeous. Assuming they had *any* compatibility at all, sex with him wouldn't be a hardship, and besides, she'd rather have Charlie and a cup of tea and a good conversation than mind-blowing sex every night.

She'd been *sure* of that. Which was why she was now so confused by the fact she couldn't stop imagining Giles Fairfax naked.

Naked and inside her, to be precise.

Naked and inside her, holding her hands down on the mattress as he moved above her, her legs wrapped around his waist as she arched her back to get closer to him, her whole body trembling with the feel of his skin against hers…

It was incredibly distracting.

Had Charlie suspected? Oh, maybe not that she'd develop this crush on her best man. But that their impending nuptials would send her a little sex-crazy, perhaps. Was he having the same problem up in Scotland?

It felt like something she should be able to discuss with her best friend—but at the same time something incredibly weird to talk to her fiancé about.

But they *had* agreed not to feel guilty if the opportunity for a last fling presented itself. So why was she feeling so guilty about even contemplating one?

Because it's Giles.

Giles, who would always be in their life. Giles, who had been her competition for so many years. Giles, who had stepped up and taken on everything Charlie had run out on in planning this wedding.

When Charlie had suggested the whole 'last fling' thing, she hadn't worried, because she'd been so sure that neither of them could want anybody else more than they wanted the future they planned together. There was no risk of anything turning serious, because Charlie's heart still belonged to Octavia, and she wanted security far more than passion.

Giles was passion. But he was also the one who'd been there for her over the weeks since Charlie had left for Scotland. The man she was getting to know in her fiancé's absence was so much more than passion.

And this was more than a crush.

That was the problem.

The tea brewed, she carried two mugs back through to the living room and plonked one on the coffee table. Giles swiped a pile of invitations out of the way just in time, as a small wave of tea escaped over the top of the mug. Millie dived for a cloth to clean it up, before slumping back down onto the sofa and staring balefully at the remaining envelopes, still unaddressed and unstamped.

If ever there was something to silence the libido, it had to be putting wedding invitations into envelopes.

And yet here Giles was, dutifully helping without a single complaint. Even though Tabby had said that the printers they used could have done the mailing, using the designer's files and some fancy mail-merge tech. Millie was the one who'd insisted on doing it by hand—partly because that felt more real, somehow, and partly to make sure that Tabby hadn't slipped any names back onto the guest list.

'You really didn't have to come and help me with this tonight,' she said.

Giles shrugged as he stuffed another envelope. 'Honestly? I didn't have anything better to do. And I promised Charlie—'

'I think this goes above and beyond best man duties,' Millie broke in. 'It's making me feel bad. Isn't there anything I could do to help you in return?'

'Actually, there is one thing.'

Giles looked up and met her gaze, and the sudden flare of heat between them caught her unaware. God, he could ask her for anything in this moment and she'd probably say yes. She wondered if he knew that.

She moistened her lips. 'Anything.'

She had to admit she wasn't expecting his reply to be, 'Go toy shopping with me.'

Her mind stuttered, drawn to a place it really shouldn't be going. A place where it was already spending too much time.

'For my niece and nephew,' he clarified, looking back down at the envelope in his hand. 'I never have any idea what to buy them for Christmas, and somehow I feel like you'll be much better at it than I would. Maybe we could go next week? Or the week after that? If there aren't too many wedding things you need to be doing.'

Actual toys. For actual children.

Right.

Mind out of the gutter, Myles.

'Sure,' she said, far more brightly than she felt. 'I can do that! Uh, I'll check the shop rota and let you know when works.'

After all, the man needed help. If that meant she got to spend a little more time lusting after his broad shoulders and handsome face before she got married, that was a cross she was willing to bear.

But that was all. She was putting this whole thing firmly back in its crush box.

Because she really couldn't let it be anything more.

Piccadilly Circus during the Christmas shopping season was, predictably, like Piccadilly Circus. Which was to say manic and chaotic, full of people who didn't quite know where they were going, and not somewhere Giles would ever choose to be if it weren't for the fact that he'd made plans to meet Millie here.

God, he was pathetic. And so far gone over a woman he couldn't dream of touching that it was ridiculous. He'd even started bargaining with himself...promising himself that as long as he didn't touch her, or tell her how he felt, he could just look and soak in the brightness that seemed to surround her, as much as possible between now and the wedding.

He knew he'd have to stop doing even that much once Charlie was back. He'd guess what was going on in Giles's head in a heartbeat. Even if he wasn't willing to admit it to himself.

This had been so much easier when he'd just wanted to sleep with her.

Giles shoved his hands in the pockets of his black wool coat and wished he'd remembered to bring gloves. Or a scarf. He wasn't really used to being outside in this sort of temperature these days. Used to be he and Charlie would be rowing, or playing rugby, or even hiking, no matter what the weather. These days he hardly seemed to leave his office, his car or his apartment. The closest he'd got to nature in a while was the greenery in Millie's shop.

Maybe he should consider moving out to a village, too. Closer to the countryside. Fresh air.

But closer to his parents, potentially, too. And no one to share it with.

Maybe he'd stay where he was.

Just as he was stamping his feet to keep some blood circulating in them he saw a berry-red bobble hat emerge from the tube station, and Millie's beaming smile follow right after. And suddenly he didn't feel so cold, or so annoyed, nor frustrated by the tourists any longer.

'Are you ready for this?' Millie bounced on her toes as she stood in front of him, gloved hands clasped by her stomach. 'The world's oldest and possibly largest toy shop, right before Christmas? It's going to be an experience!'

'Hmm…' Giles replied, noncommittally. 'You realise it would have been closer if we'd met at Oxford Circus?'

Millie shrugged. 'I know. But I just love the walk up Regent Street. And we can end up on Oxford Street to see the lights!'

'I suppose we can.'

Why wasn't he surprised that she'd thought

this through? Somehow, Millie managed to make things an *experience*, rather than a chore. He already felt his mood lifting—and was surprisingly annoyed by it.

Regent Street was, he had to admit, beautiful in the late-afternoon winter light. The sun was already sinking behind the pale stone of the crescent, and the twinkly overhead Christmas lights were coming on. And walking beside Millie, watching her joy in the moment, made him feel almost joyous, too.

He could just keep walking with her, commenting on the city at Christmas, all night. But before very long he saw the red awnings of Hamleys stretching out over the pavement, beckoning in toy-shoppers from far and wide.

They stopped in front of the store and stared up at it together.

Seven floors of toys. Seven floors of people Christmas shopping. What on earth had he been thinking?

'We can hold hands if you're scared,' Millie said drily.

'Terrified,' he admitted. 'But I'm pretending to be brave in front of you.'

She laughed. 'I really wouldn't bother. I like you scared—it makes you more human. Come on.'

Suddenly she grabbed his hand in her own gloved one and pulled him past the shop assistants demonstrating the latest toys, dragging him towards the escalator.

'I'm assuming you don't want to go the boring stuffed toy route?' she said, as they rose up to the next floor. 'So, what are the kids into? How old are they, again?'

'Benjy is seven and Lily is nine,' he said, glad he'd checked their ages with his sister by text while he was waiting for Millie. 'Lily likes… craft stuff, I think? And Benjy…'

He had no idea. He only knew about the crafts because last time he'd visited—well, last time he'd visited when the kids were awake—he'd been presented with some sort of card decorated with curled paper and glue that had stuck to his jacket.

'Is seven,' Millie finished for him. 'So he would probably want *everything* in this shop.'

'Probably,' he agreed, with a chuckle. 'So, where do we start?'

'At the top!' Millie tugged him towards the next escalator. 'We start at the top and work our way down. Okay?'

'Sure.' Giles shrugged.

What else could he say?

Millie took over from there. They enjoyed the trains going around and around an elaborate track, considered the models and drones as they moved down the store, pausing for a while at the remote-control vehicles. Giles might have chased her around with one of the display models, until one of the shop assistants stepped in, but she got her own back with the army of talking cuddly bear creatures she set on him.

The arts and crafts section on the third floor furnished him with a whole armful of things for Lily—from colour-changing pens to stamps to pastels, and plenty of paper to use them on. He also placed an order for an easel to be delivered later.

They continued down to examine the board games, before heading back up again to purchase the remote-control car he'd really wanted for Benjy from the start.

'You can drive it with him on Christmas morning!'

Millie sounded so excited at the prospect that he didn't have the heart to tell her he probably wouldn't actually see the children on the day. They'd be with Rebekah's husband's family, as always.

Laden down with bags, they finally left Hamleys and continued to walk up towards Oxford Street. By now dark had fallen fully and the Christmas lights sparkled brightly overhead, lighting up the skies with festive wonder.

Normally Giles would walk under them, head down, barely noticing their sparkle. With Millie holding on to his arm, that wasn't even an option.

He saw every light, every joyous moment, reflected in her eyes.

He swallowed and looked away.

This was more than a problem. This was a disaster.

He wanted his best friend's fiancée. And not only couldn't he have her, he *shouldn't*. Everything she wanted from her future was the opposite to what he needed.

When he thought about it that way, it really was just as well she was engaged to someone else. And to the one person he could never dream of betraying at that. Charlie would give her the future she wanted. What could he possibly offer her?

Four and a half weeks until the wedding. And he already knew every second of them was going to be unbearable.

'Okay?' Millie squeezed his arm and smiled up at him.

He smiled back before he could stop himself. 'Just fine,' he lied.

He was always fine. That was how he got by.

And he'd get through this, too.

Just four and a half more weeks.

CHAPTER NINE

THE WREATH-MAKING WORKSHOP she ran every year in the back room of Holly and Ivy was Millie's favourite festive activity outside of Christmas week itself. She wasn't a huge fan of Christmas shopping—toy shopping with Giles had been an exception to that rule—and while she enjoyed a Christmas advert, or receiving her first card, it was the wreath-making workshop in early December that always made her start to feel properly Christmassy.

Greenery and berries and chicken wire and bows were neatly gathered in vases and piles on each table, and Millie had the coffee maker brewing and pastries from the local bakery on hand for everyone. This year, she had more people signed up than ever, and the tables with supplies reached from the back room into the shop itself to accommodate everybody.

And that was before the extra walk-in arrived…just before she was due to open the doors to her paid-up participants.

The shadow at the door grabbed her attention—although until she got closer she assumed it was someone early for the workshop. When she saw who it really was, she yanked the door open and beckoned him inside, out of the cold.

'Giles! I wasn't expecting you today, was I?' She had to admit, with everything that was going on with wedding prep and the business, she wasn't *quite* as on top of her calendar the way she'd like to be.

He gave her a forgiving smile. 'I was just passing. Tabby asked me to drop these off for you.'

She took the large padded envelope from his hand and opened it. 'You've been up at Howard Hall?'

'I was up that way, sorting some things at my family estate. I dropped by to give her a rundown on the wedding stuff, since she wouldn't stop texting me—apparently you've stopped replying?' Giles sniffed. 'Is that coffee?'

'Mmm, help yourself.' She motioned towards the coffee machine. 'I was *going* to reply, but I've just been so busy getting ready for today's wreath-making workshop. Want to join in?'

It was an impulse to ask him—a foolish one, really. But she'd had one last-minute cancellation-due-to-illness email that morning so there was space…just about. And now he was here she was sort of loath to let him just go again, before they'd even talked or anything.

When had she got so dependent on having him around? She wasn't sure, but she had to admit that it had happened. And, as much as she knew it was a terrible idea with Charlie away, it felt good to have him on her side.

And *by* her side, too.

'Wreath-making?' Giles frowned a little, but then shrugged and said, 'Sure.'

'Great.'

They did a little awkward dance—him making and then drinking coffee, while she finished setting up for the workshop—until the other participants arrived. After that she was too busy running the show—tweaking chicken wire, arranging berries and advising people on leaf placement—to worry too much about Giles. She was barely even surprised, when she stopped by his station, to see that he'd turned out a more than serviceable wreath. He seemed to be competent at almost everything he turned his hand to.

It was more of a turn-on than she cared to admit.

Everything Giles Fairfax did these days seemed to turn her on, though. She could hardly believe she'd come to this, given the animosity between them as teens, but there it was. She *wanted* him—every single inch of him—pressed up against her. As often as possible…

Wait. What was she meant to be doing? Right, wreath workshop.

Focus, Myles.

'Okay, so if you take one of the stems with berries on…'

Even when it was over, and her happy students were leaving with their wreaths, chatting and possibly heading over to the pub, by the sound of things, Giles didn't leave. Instead, he stayed to help her clear up, sweeping up clippings and bits of ribbon efficiently.

Millie found herself watching him rather than doing her own chores, mesmerised by the way the muscles in his forearms flexed as he worked. How his hair flopped over his forehead and he flipped it out of the way. The way he carefully moved his own wreath to clear underneath it. How he'd taken the workshop utterly seriously, despite the fact she was almost certain it wasn't how he'd choose to spend his day off.

But he'd come, and he'd stayed anyway. Why?

Why was he doing all this? Could it really be just because of his promise to Charlie?

She tried to convince herself that it was. That he was just a really, really good friend. That she was imagining the way she caught him watching her sometimes. Those times she only caught him because she was already watching him.

And again and again that last conversation with Charlie kept returning to haunt her. His assurances that if she needed to let loose a little before the wedding he was fine with that.

She wasn't sure she was, though.

But maybe she was just being prudish about this. Maybe if she got this crush out of her system somehow, she'd be able to settle down to the future she'd chosen with Charlie. Passion wasn't love, after all—and it certainly wasn't for ever. She *knew* that.

But passion was definitely what she wanted with Giles. She could barely think about anything else these days. It would scare her, if it were anyone else. But she knew she could trust Giles. And it wasn't as if he could break her heart if everything was on her terms—she'd be the one walking away to marry another man.

She didn't want to go into marriage with any regrets. And Giles had already told her flat that he had no interest in the kind of future she wanted, so anything between them could only be casual.

A pre-wedding fling.

Would that be so terrible?

Of course it would mean admitting the truth to Giles. Telling him everything. She wasn't sure *that* was what Charlie had had in mind when he'd given her the out for 'a fling before the ring'.

But if it was the only way to shake these feelings—this uncertain *wanting* that kept her awake at night, that had her thinking more about Giles's arms around her than her wedding planning… Charlie was her best friend. He'd understand.

Wouldn't he?

Would Giles, though? Would he despise her for marrying without love in the traditional, romantic sense, anyway? She knew how he felt about marriage. Wasn't she just proving him right? That it was all transactional, anyway?

Would he put those feelings aside if it meant they could give in to the pressure building between them?

She supposed there was only one way to find out.

'I think we're done.'

Giles leant the broom against the wall and turned to find Millie by the door, staring at him. When he caught her, she turned away and locked the door.

What was happening here?

'Don't I need to leave through that?' He spoke lightly, hoping to cover his uncertainty.

'Later.'

Millie's voice didn't even sound like hers. It was rougher, and filled with a sort of fearful excitement he didn't know what to make of.

'I need to talk to you about something first. Want a cup of tea before you go?'

Okay, tea. That was good. If something was really wrong she'd be offering him alcohol. But he couldn't shake the feeling that something wasn't quite right, either. That something was about to change, dramatically, and all he could do was sit back and let it happen.

'Sure.'

He handed her the broom and watched as she put it away in a cupboard, then followed her up the stairs to her little flat—a place that was becoming far more familiar to him than it probably should.

Soon, mugs in hand, they were both perched on opposite sides of her coffee table and Giles was waiting for her to start. Millie, meanwhile, was chewing so violently on her lower lip that he was afraid she might do permanent damage.

'So?' he asked. 'What did you want to talk to me about? Is it to do with the wedding?'

'In a way,' Millie replied. 'I mean, yes. Completely, in some ways. And in others...' She looked down at her mug.

Well, that cleared everything right up. He was going to have to get a Millie translator in here at this rate. Her babbling was endearing, but not exactly informative.

'You realise you're not making a lot of sense here?' he said, gently.

She looked down again. 'I know. I just... This is kind of hard to say. So...be patient with me?'

'Of course.' He sat back, his mind whirring with possibilities. 'Take your time.'

He wasn't even sure what he hoped she'd say. If he wanted this to be about...well, about them, or not. Confirmation that he wasn't the only one feeling this way would be nice, but on the other hand it would only open up a whole different box of problems.

She loved Charlie. She was marrying Charlie.

And he was never getting married at all.

So what good would it do anyway?

Whatever he was expecting, it wasn't what she started with.

'I saw the doctor a few months ago, and he gave me some…unexpected news.'

Giles's heart clenched, and in that moment he'd have done anything—*anything*—to make sure she was okay. But all he could actually do was reach across the divide between them and take her hand.

'What news?'

'My fertility is declining—fast. And I've always wanted a family. I was an only child, and I want…more. I found out just before Octavia's wedding.'

'Just before you got engaged to Charlie.'

He trusted Millie, and believed she was a good person—possibly the best person he'd met since Charlie. But he couldn't ignore that coincidence of timing.

'Does he know?'

She nodded. 'I told him that night. And he told me that, with Octavia Mrs Layton Stone now, he couldn't see himself ever finding someone else to marry. Except he needs to, because of the estate and the family name and everything.'

Things were becoming horribly clear—in a way that Giles really wished they wouldn't.

'So you put the moves on him? Convinced him to marry *you* so you can have your family?' He pulled away. 'Did you ever love him at all? Is this the culmination of decades-long unrequited love, or are you just taking advantage of my best friend in his weakest moment?'

She recoiled as if he'd slapped her. 'Is that what you think of me?'

Giles closed his eyes and pressed his hands to them, his mug of tea forgotten on the coffee table. 'No,' he admitted. 'It's not. Not at all. But I just don't understand where this is going.'

'Then stop accusing me of things and start listening,' she said sharply. 'You've always listened before. Don't ruin it now.'

He nodded, and stayed silent.

The story of how Millie and Charlie's engagement had come to be flowed over him, and he knew he'd be processing it for hours, even days to come. But for now, only one part really stood out.

'You lied to me. You *both* lied to me.'

'Not really.'

Millie's face was drawn, tired and strained in a way he'd never seen before—not even when she'd been arguing with Tabby about wedding guest lists.

'We *do* love each other. It might not be the kind of romantic love you read about in books, but it's real and it's ours. We love and care for each other more than anyone else in the world, and we've decided to spend our lives together, to have a family together, and to live in happy, friendly harmony together. What's wrong with that?'

She made it sound reasonable, and he had to admit that they probably had a stronger base to work from than most married couples he'd stood up with in the past few years. Certainly more than any in his own family.

But still…

'What about passion? Attraction, at least? You're going to have to get those babies somehow, you realise?'

He just couldn't imagine someone as vibrantly alive as Millie living without the kind of passion she deserved in her life.

'We know. We've discussed it.'

She sat so primly on her chair that he couldn't help but wonder how, exactly, those discussions had gone.

'And?'

'Once we're married, we will be…intimate. And only with each other. This isn't going to be one of those fake marriages where they both pretend to be in love but actually have other partners on the side. Once we say *I do* we're both all in. He'll be the only man I ever sleep with.'

There was something about the way she said it... Or perhaps it was in the way she met his gaze as she spoke. Or how she leaned a little closer across the table, maybe.

Whatever it was, the room suddenly felt smaller. Warmer. The air was heavy with a tension he couldn't quite understand—until he thought back over her words.

'Once we're married... Once we say I do...'

'What about *before* the wedding?'

The words were out before he could fully consider what it meant for him to be saying them. Where they could lead.

Where he even wanted them to lead.

'Charlie has made it clear that until the wedding, if either of us have something we need to... to get out of our systems, say, then we should do that.'

She wasn't meeting his gaze any longer. She was staring down at her hands to avoid looking at him.

And suddenly, finally, Giles understood why she'd brought him to her flat tonight.

He just wasn't quite sure yet what he was going to do about it.

Millie didn't like the way Giles was looking at her. As if something had changed in her appearance and he was trying to figure out what. Or as if he wasn't sure she was the person he'd thought she was.

He was re-evaluating everything he knew about her—she could tell. And she didn't know how he would feel once he'd finished.

There was nothing she could do about it. She'd put her cards on the table, and now she had to wait. She'd been honest—more honest than she was really comfortable with. Now she had to wait and see if he'd be honest in return.

She figured he had three options.

One, he'd thank her for telling him, pretend it had no personal impact on him, finish his tea and leave.

Two, he'd say he understood, and admit to the draw between them, but then remind her that Charlie was his best friend and they'd be seeing each other in that capacity for the rest of their lives once she and Charlie were married, and he didn't want to complicate that for them all.

Three… Well, three was the one she was placing all her hopes on.

If she were honest, she expected him to go for Two, though. He'd always been straight with her, and she couldn't imagine he'd try to pretend that her feelings were all one-sided.

Unless they really were and she'd read this all wrong…

Oh, God, *why* wasn't he talking yet? She'd had

time to reason all this out in her brain and he hadn't even said a word yet!

Finally, *finally* his mouth opened. Then closed again. Then he spoke.

'I… I'm not sure what to say to that, if I'm honest. In some ways it explains a lot. I mean, the way you two went from friends to fiancés overnight… I kind of worried about that a bit. And I'm glad I *do* know. But in other ways…it doesn't really change anything at all.'

'Doesn't change anything?' Millie felt her hopes sinking as she repeated his words.

'Because Charlie is my best friend. My one and only constant for the last God knows how many years. And I can't… Millie, I can't do anything to ruin that. No matter how tempting it might be.'

His gaze met hers and her breath caught in her chest. 'But it is…tempting?'

Giles looked away and swore quietly. When he looked up at her again Millie saw an intensity in his eyes she'd never seen in him before. Heat flooded across her body at having that focus all on her.

'Millie, if you think for a moment that I haven't spent every day since the wedding holding back from telling you how much I want you…all the bloody time…then you are sorely mistaken.'

Oh, God. It wasn't just her. It really was both of them. She hadn't imagined the electricity between them. Or the heat that was flooding her body at his words.

Now the only question was what they were going to do about it.

Giles thought he'd made up his mind. But Millie didn't think he'd thought through all the possibilities just yet.

'What if it didn't have to ruin anything?'

Millie's voice was breathy and low, and Giles's blood pounded at the sound of it. At the possibility in it. At what it might mean for both of them.

He should leave.

He should have left already.

But wild horses couldn't have dragged him from this place right now.

He swallowed. 'What are you suggesting?'

Millie leaned closer over the coffee table and Giles was torn between pulling away, and saving his sanity, and moving in closer and giving himself everything he wanted.

'I want my future with Charlie. I want a secure and stable and loving family with lots of kids. I could take or leave the big house and the family line, but I can't deny that the security of the money is good. But that's not why I'm doing this. I'm marrying him for the family it will give me—and to give him what he needs to live his life the way he wants, too. He's my best friend and we're going to be happy together.'

'Okay. But none of that is explaining how something between you and me wouldn't ruin it,' Giles admitted.

'Because you *don't* want any of those things,' Millie pointed out. 'Nothing between us could ever become serious enough to endanger the plans Charlie and I have made. We couldn't fall in love and call off the wedding because that goes against everything you want, and I could never love someone who doesn't want the same things as me.'

'Okay, so what are you suggesting?'

Giles's head was spinning with all the contradictions. She didn't love Charlie, but she loved the idea of marrying him. She *desired* Giles, it seemed, but not the life *he* wanted. So what *did* she want, really?

'A pre-wedding fling,' she said bluntly. 'No expectations, no *feelings*, even. Just…scratching an itch.'

'No, really, stop…you're embarrassing me with your flattery,' he replied in a monotone.

Millie rolled her eyes. 'You know what I mean. You don't love me. You don't *want* to love me. And nothing that happens between us is going to change your feelings about marriage, is it?'

'No.'

That much, at least, he was sure about. Everything else seemed to be shifting sands.

'And I want my future with Charlie too much

to risk it by engaging in anything more than a fling with you,' she said simply. 'But... I can't ignore this feeling between us, either. I've tried—trust me, I've tried.'

'So have I,' he admitted.

'I know that passion...chemistry...doesn't equal love or for ever. It's just sex. It's far safer than love. So I figure the best thing to do is to get it out of our systems before the wedding,' Millie explained. 'I mean, it would only be worse if we kept on feeling this way *after* I was married, wouldn't it?'

'That's true.'

He was certain there was a flaw in her logic somewhere, but he was struggling to see it right now. Was that because she was right or just because he was hypnotised by her eyes.

'I haven't... Since I broke up with my last boyfriend—and that was a while ago—I haven't been with anyone. I might even have forgotten how, it's been so long. And it would be...useful to have a reminder before I get married.'

'So this is purely practical?'

He raised an eyebrow at her and she blushed, shaking her head a little.

'No. It's not. I just... I want this. I want to settle down and have the life I've planned with Charlie. But I also want *you*. I want to enjoy these last weeks before the wedding, and I want to see where this connection leads. Don't you?'

Her eyes shone with determination as she met his gaze, and he could see the fire behind them. The passion.

And, God, he wanted to taste it. Taste her.

Giles didn't have it in him to deny it any longer.

So, instead of answering, he leant forward and captured her lips with his own.

CHAPTER TEN

MILLIE WOKE UP ALONE.

To be fair, she'd gone to bed alone, too. After that kiss she'd had expectations—high ones, given the way that just the press of Giles's lips against hers had made her entire body tingle. She'd thought—hoped—that they'd moved past the awkward conversation part now that she'd bared her soul and exposed her biggest secret, and could move on to the much more fun, physical part.

But it had turned out that Giles had other ideas about what happened next.

He'd pulled away and rested his forehead against hers, his breath coming as fast as her own. 'As much as I want to take this further, I also think we need to be careful.'

'And what does being "careful" mean?' she'd asked, hoping it was a question of contraception rather than anything more serious.

She'd needed him. Now she'd finally admitted how much, she *really* hadn't wanted to wait.

But she'd been disappointed.

'It means we take tonight to be sure,' he'd replied. 'This has moved fast—for me, at least. An hour ago I thought you were madly, passionately in love with Charlie, remember? This whole… arrangement is a lot to digest. So we take tonight to make sure we're both certain about this. And in the morning we can lay some ground rules, if we're still both sure.'

It had been so much like the night she and Charlie had first had the idea of getting married… She couldn't exactly say no—not when she knew he was right.

So she'd given him blankets and pillows for the sofa and retreated to her own bed, frustrated and confused and wondering what the morning would bring.

And now it was here.

They were *supposed* to be visiting the Christmas markets in the nearby town, to search for wedding favours that would satisfy both her *and* Tabby's tastes, but Millie had a feeling that they weren't going to be top priority for the day.

That went to the conversation they really, really needed to have.

She slipped out of bed and into the bathroom next door, so she could at least clean her teeth and sort her hair before facing him. What if he'd come to his senses and decided the whole thing was crazy?

She *knew* it was crazy. But *she* was going crazy not having him, so it still seemed like the lesser of two evils. This was what passion did to a person—and why she wasn't going to base her whole future on it. But the next few weeks? That…that she wanted. With Giles.

Huh. She'd slept on it, like he'd asked, and she still wanted this. This last chance to cut loose—with him—before marriage.

But he'd also wanted her to think about rules, so she considered that as she brushed her teeth, and by the time she emerged into the lounge she had a pretty good idea of what she needed from this arrangement.

She found Giles sitting warily on her sofa, wearing boxers and a thin T-shirt, two cups of tea in front of him.

'I heard you get up,' he said, by way of explanation.

From the way he was watching her—as if he expected her to dart away and run off down the stairs at any moment—he thought she had changed her mind. Or he had. She guessed it was time to find out which.

'I've been thinking,' she said. 'Like you told me to.'

'And you've changed your mind?'

She shook her head. 'I've figured out how this needs to work, to make sure it doesn't ruin anything.'

He pushed her tea towards her as she sat town. 'Tell me. Because I've been thinking all night and...'

He did look tired. Like, bone-tired and worn out.

'And?'

'And I'm scared, Millie. I want this—want *you*—badly. I can admit that. But this is exactly why I stay away from serious relationships. I can't... My life, my plans, will only work if I'm only worrying about myself. I can't add another person into the mix.'

'You don't need to,' she reassured him. 'I am absolutely not your problem, okay? Look, here's what I was thinking. We need ground rules—you were right about that—and these are mine. This is a last-ditch fling for me—nothing more. It is all over when Charlie gets home...before we head up for the wedding. No one gets attached and we stay friends afterwards—that one really matters, because against all my best efforts I actually *like* you now you're not an idiot teenage boy any more, and I don't want to lose you as a friend.'

He looked slightly poleaxed at that, but smiled a little shyly and said, 'Okay...'

'This is the big one, though,' she went on. 'Nobody knows. I don't want anyone thinking that my marriage to Charlie isn't true love in the traditional way—especially not his parents or my mother or Tabby. So we keep this secret. Can you do that?'

Giles reached across the table and took her hand in his, keeping his gaze fixed on her own. Millie couldn't help but recognise how different this felt from her similar conversation with Charlie just a couple of months ago.

With Charlie she'd felt safe and secure, even if she'd been a little nervous, because he was her best friend and she knew he'd never hurt her. She'd looked into his eyes and felt comforted and comfortable, too.

With Giles… She met his gaze and her whole body felt on edge, sparking as if electricity was racing through her blood. This wasn't comfortable—it was terrifying.

But exciting, too.

'I can do that,' Giles said, his voice low. 'And your rules are my rules, too. Everything I decided during the night.'

'Then it seems like we're in sync on this.'

On more than this, she was willing to bet, if only he'd kiss her again.

'We are,' he said.

She wasn't sure which of them moved first, but suddenly there was no coffee table between them—no distance at all, in fact—and she was in his arms, kissing him again, and it felt even better than it had the night before.

Eventually, they pulled apart again.

'So, we have a deal, then?' she asked breathlessly.

'An arrangement,' Giles countered. 'Just until Charlie comes home.'

'Exactly. And in that case… I think the Christmas markets can wait, don't you?'

Even getting to the bedroom seemed like an insurmountable challenge. But taking Millie for the first time on her sofa, with one or other of them banging into the coffee table, wasn't a great plan. Giles decided that compromise was the way forward, stripping her pyjama top slowly from her as she lay back on the sofa, and taking his time savouring every inch he uncovered one by one.

She squirmed a little under him as he kissed his way up her ribcage. 'Tickles?'

'Mmm.' Millie looked down at him with hooded eyes. 'But in a good way. Don't stop.'

'I really wasn't planning to.' His next kiss brushed the underside of her breast, and this time she shuddered rather than squirmed. 'Definitely not now…'

Another inch or so and he'd uncovered the rosy tips of her nipples—first the right, then the left—taking them each in his mouth in turn, delighting in the way she arched up to meet him, and how they hardened even more under his tongue.

This—this was what he needed. What he'd been wanting since Millie Myles had come back into his life again and they'd danced at the wedding. The chance to get to know her—completely. The last two months of wedding planning had introduced him to her mind, her personality, in a way years of competing over Charlie's friendship never had. And now, finally, he had the chance to get to know her body, too. He didn't intend to waste a moment of it.

'Giles…'

The sound of his name on her lips, the desperate way her hips canted up to meet his—all conspired to force him into action.

But he made himself take his time.

He did finish taking off her pyjamas, though, stripping the top from her shoulders before sliding the pyjama pants down her shapely legs. He had to pause, to take a moment to regain control as all that bare flesh came into view, though. Then he pulled off his own T-shirt and got to work.

This time he started lower, parting her thighs and kneeling between them, kissing his way up to her core, desperate to know, to taste, to feel this most secret part of her. She tensed under him for just a moment and he stopped, waiting for her to relax again or ask him to stop.

When she did neither, he risked a glance up and found her watching him. 'Do you want this?' he asked.

Her throat bobbed as she swallowed, then finally she said, 'More than I can remember wanting anything, right now.'

And that was all the answer he needed.

Millie felt every muscle in her body clench as Giles's tongue swept over her, and she reached down to tangle her fingers in his hair—not to hold him there, but to be part of what he was doing. To show him how *much* she was part of this, too.

It wasn't something he was doing *to* her.

It was something they were doing together.

Together, they'd fallen into this. And now Millie knew she wouldn't be able to bear being apart from him again until they had to say goodbye for good.

She was going to suck every single moment of pleasure, of togetherness, from this fling before she started her real life again.

Then Giles shifted slightly, changed the angle of his tongue on her body, and every rational thought flew from her brain. She didn't have thoughts any longer, only feelings. Senses... Senses that felt as if they were about to spark and catch fire if she couldn't—

Her orgasm burst through her in waves of electric beauty, and she swore she actually saw coloured lights behind her eyes.

It had *definitely* never been like that with any of her exes.

It'll probably never be like that with Charlie, either.

The thought brought her down faster than she'd have liked. She pushed it away. That was why she was going to make the most of this time now. And who knew? If she learned enough about what made her explode like that, maybe she'd be able to teach her new husband one day, even if the thought of that conversation made her squirm.

Funny how she'd always thought she and Charlie could talk about anything. But *this?* She wasn't sure.

Giles rested his cheek against her stomach and gazed up at her. 'Did I lose you?'

'No. God, no. I just…needed a minute.' She reached down to trace a finger along his shoulder. 'And now I've had it…do you want to try this in an actual bed?'

'Sounds good to me.'

In an instant he was on his feet, yanking her up from the sofa and pulling her close against him. He still wore his boxers, but nothing else, and she could feel him hard and hot and *big* through the fabric.

'God, I want you,' she breathed, her brain not bothering to filter the words before they reached her mouth.

She'd expected a smug smirk in response, but instead Giles looked serious, and dipped his head to press a hard, fast kiss to her lips.

'Not half as much as I want you right now. Watching you fall apart like that... Millie...'

She swallowed. 'Bedroom. Now.'

She didn't want to talk. They'd done talking... done getting to know each other.

All she wanted to do now was feel. And make the most of having this man in her bed and her arms before she had to say goodbye.

Eventually, they made it out to the Christmas markets.

The town they'd chosen—less than an hour's drive from Millie's little village—clearly made a big deal about Christmas, and it was probably a good boost to the economy, too, since the place was buzzing even in the fading late-afternoon sunlight.

Bright white lights were strung across narrow cobbled streets, with cosy-looking shops decorated for the season peeking out from under ancient roofs and between wooden beams. In the market square, stalls that looked like miniature log cabins had been set up in a horseshoe shape, selling everything from glass ornaments and hand-carved nutcrackers to Santa hats and sleigh bells.

The open end of the horseshoe led to the local pub, which seemed to be doing a roaring trade in spiced cider, mulled wine and cones of chips eaten straight from the paper with plenty of salt and vinegar. Just the smell was making Giles's mouth water.

They hadn't exactly stopped to eat much that morning. Or at lunchtime. They'd had other priorities. And Giles was not regretting those choices.

Holding Millie in his arms, kissing her, feeling her skin against his own, his body claiming hers... He'd choose that over and over again if he could. Especially knowing that their time alone together was limited, and growing shorter all the time. In just a few short weeks the wedding would be upon them and they'd go back to being friends, so for now he'd take advantage of every moment they had.

'Do you know anyone in this town?' he asked softly.

'Nope,' Millie replied. 'Not a soul.'

'In that case...' He took her gloved hand in his own, holding it tightly as they perused the stalls.

Holding hands with a woman wasn't something he usually craved, or even liked, but it was different with Millie. Probably because he knew this was his only chance.

Together they studied the festive fare on offer, considering its suitability as table presents or favours for the wedding guests. Giles suspected they were cutting it rather fine on finding the right thing, but since Millie and Tabby had been disagreeing on the matter almost since the engagement had been announced, he was keen to help Millie find something she liked, so she didn't have to give in to Tabby and go with her preferred supplier of…whatever the hell it was Charlie's sister wanted on the tables. Giles had to admit he'd given up on listening to the particulars a few weeks before.

'What do you think of these?' Millie asked, as they paused at one of the log cabin stalls. 'I think they could work.'

Giles studied the hand-carved decorations. Despite being made from wood, they were delicate as the snowflakes they depicted, each tied on a dark red or green ribbon, and looking for all the world as if they might fall from the leaden sky above.

'I think they're perfect,' he agreed. 'Now let's see if they have enough of the things…'

Luckily they did—just. Millie bought up more or less the whole stock—making the artist's day in the process—and sent a photo to Tabby, presenting the whole thing as a *fait accompli*. Hopefully Charlie's sister would like them as much as Millie and Giles did, but really, it wasn't *actually* her wedding anyway.

Giles stopped halfway through packing the carefully wrapped snowflakes into a bag.

Of course it wasn't *his* wedding, either.

For a moment there he'd forgotten. He'd got so caught up in the wedding planning, in helping and supporting Millie, that he'd actually *forgotten* he wasn't the groom here—only the best man.

He finished packing the bag and stepped away, clutching it safely, leaving Millie to finish chatting with the artist. He needed space and air. He needed to breathe—and to think.

Because it wasn't just the wedding planning, was it? It was being with Millie. Not just in the way they had been that morning—naked and entwined. But spending time with her. Talking and laughing with her. Listening to her points of view and having her listen to his.

He'd never had a friendship or a relationship like this before. If this was how things were for her and Charlie, no wonder his best friend had jumped at the chance to marry Millie. If marriage could be like this…

But it couldn't. Not for him.

'You okay with those?' Millie appeared beside him, pink-cheeked and smiling, gesturing towards the bag of snowflakes. 'I can take them.'

He clutched the bag closer and shook his head. 'Come on. If we're done shopping, let's go and get some of those chips and some spiced cider.'

'I am never going to disagree with that plan,' Millie said cheerfully.

She bounded off in the direction of the pub and Giles followed more slowly, still thinking.

He'd never told Millie quite why he was so opposed to the idea of marriage. But for the first time he wanted to.

If he could only figure out how.

CHAPTER ELEVEN

MILLIE WASN'T SURE what had changed while they were at the Christmas markets, but something definitely had. Either Giles secretly really hated the wedding favours they'd chosen, or he was having second thoughts about their arrangement.

He'd been subdued over chips and spiced cider, but the atmosphere in the pub had made up for that—and really, they'd hardly been able to hear each other talk anyway, so she hadn't thought much of it.

But he'd been silent for almost all of the journey home, and when she'd mentioned that they couldn't be too far from his own family home a line had settled between his eyebrows that hadn't gone away for the rest of the drive.

Was *that* it? Something to do with his parents or his sister distracting him? She'd like to think so, but she wasn't convinced. He hadn't even *looked* at her on the drive back to her flat above the shop.

He'd followed her up the stairs, though—that

was something. She'd half expected him to say goodbye at the door and drive back to London, even though it was getting late.

By the time she'd put her key in the door she'd convinced herself that he'd decided the whole fling idea was a mistake and she'd never get to kiss him again. Let alone feel him moving inside her, his lips over every inch of her body…which, after everything she'd experienced that morning, would be a crying shame.

And, actually, she wasn't going to let him make that decision without talking to her about it. They'd *both* set the rules they were playing by. They *both* got to decide when they changed.

The door opened and she stepped inside, turning around immediately to confront him. But before she was able to get a word out he'd spun her around, backing her up against the closing door, his mouth on hers.

The warmth of her anger rapidly transformed into a passionate heat, flooding her senses and making her skin tingle. She waited for him to say something—maybe about how he'd been imagining this all the way home, and that was why he'd seemed so focussed—but he didn't. He didn't say anything at all.

His mouth never left hers as his hands roamed up under the wool of her knitted dress, her coat falling from her shoulders as he pushed the dress up and over her head, breaking their kiss just long enough to leave her in bra and tights.

'God, you're gorgeous,' he murmured, before kissing her again.

Was this really what he'd been thinking about on the drive home? She was sure she hadn't been imagining his bad mood...

'Giles... Giles!' she said against his mouth, and he pulled back, resting his forehead against hers.

'Do you want me to stop?'

His voice was low, full of wanting, and Millie's body knew her answer even before her mind did.

'God, no.'

'Then less talking, more touching.'

He kissed her again, his fingers already un-clasping her bra behind her back.

Maybe they could talk later. Right now, she had far more important things to concentrate on.

She slid her fingers under his own clothes, and lost herself in the feel of his skin instead.

Later—quite a lot later—Millie rested her head on his chest, glad they'd finally made it to her bed at last, and asked, 'So...what was all that about?'

He looked down at her with an eyebrow raised. 'I think I was fairly clear on that matter at the time. I wanted you. Badly. And it seemed you rather returned the feeling...?'

'Oh, I definitely did,' she confirmed, her body still happily tingling. 'It was just...sudden. In the car, I thought there was something wrong—I even thought you might be about to call the whole thing off. Then, when we got back—'

Giles's arm tightened around her. 'Quite the opposite. I'm just...very aware of how little time we have together. And I want to make the most of it.'

'Me too.'

She was excited for her new life with Charlie—of course she was. But she couldn't deny that saying goodbye to this...with Giles...was going to be hard. Even if it *was* only a fling. Still, they had a few weeks. Probably the chemistry would have worn off by then, and Giles would have grown bored and be ready to leave anyway.

'So...is that what you were frowning about in the car?'

Giles sighed. Then, unexpectedly, he released her from his arms and sat up against the headboard. Confused, she followed suit, and he pulled her back in against his shoulder, drawing the duvet up over them both for warmth.

'I was thinking about my parents,' he admitted. 'And my sister. And...well, marriage.'

That was *not* what Millie had been expecting.

'Marriage?' The word came out a little squeaky.

'You asked me once, do you remember? Why I'm so against the idea of marriage?'

'Yeah, I remember.'

She hadn't ever really expected him to answer, though. She'd assumed it was just the usual reasons. Not wanting to be tied down, loving freedom more than security, being scared of commitment. Or always wanting the next high—the excitement and passion that came with a new relationship without having to worry about what happened when it became stale and old because he'd already have moved on. Heaven knew she'd met enough men suffering from the same affliction—Tom being a case in point.

'That's what I was thinking of in the car. How as much as I'm enjoying being with you, and how under other circumstances this could be something more than it is, it can't. Because of them.'

This wasn't what Millie had expected at all. She could hear the pain in his voice as he spoke, the frustration. And for almost the first time she let herself wonder about the what ifs.

What if Giles *didn't* hate the idea of marriage and children?

What if she didn't have to get married *now* if she wanted a baby?

What if Charlie didn't need her to marry him, too?

But that way madness lay. Because the world was the way the world was, and they could only live in it, not change it. Not fundamentals like that.

So instead she listened.

'Tell me,' she said, shifting against his shoulder so she could watch his face as he spoke.

'My parents…theirs was a marriage of…inconvenience, I guess. Obviously I wasn't around then, but from the stories I've heard my dad fell for my mum pretty hard, but it seems the attraction was mostly physical. His parents *definitely* didn't approve, because she wasn't from their usual society set. You know how that goes.'

Millie did know. The fact that she'd been so welcomed by Charlie's family probably had a lot more to do with being the least awful option compared to Octavia than any actual pleasure in her humble upbringing. The fact that she'd at least grown up *at* Howard Hall, more or less, meant that she understood how things there worked, which she supposed was a bonus.

'My mum got pregnant, and back then and there that meant they had to get married. She was thrilled—and so was her family. I mean, she'd taken a step up in life. But they didn't know each other very well—not as well as you need to in order to get married, anyway. They had my sister and…well, it soon became clear that my mother loved the house and the title and the money more than she loved my father. And he… I don't think he loved anything at all—except maybe showing off.'

'Showing off?' Millie asked.

Giles shrugged the shoulder she wasn't leaning on. 'Best as I can figure, anyway. He spends money like it's nothing, and always on flashy things—things that say *I have a lot of money* to anyone watching. You know how they always say that the richest people *don't* flaunt their wealth? Well, by the time my dad inherited the title the estate was already in trouble. He's been pretending to be the rich lord of the manor his ancestors were ever since.'

'I bet your mum was pretty angry when she figured that out,' Millie guessed.

'I imagine she was, too,' Giles agreed. 'But they've never mentioned it. They like to keep up appearances…pretend that all is normal.'

'That sounds…unhelpful.'

'It is.' Giles sighed. 'Very.'

'So…how do they manage, then? Do they rent out the house for events, like Charlie's family?'

The way Charlie told it, his family had been on the verge of ruin—which she suspected meant a very different thing to that sphere of society than to most people—or at least of having to sell off a lot of land or property until his parents found a way to turn the family legacy into a business opportunity.

'Oh, they would never.' Giles sounded bitter about that. 'Trust me, I've tried to persuade them. But for them, they can't understand the point of being titled if it doesn't entitle them to exactly the kind of life they want. And that doesn't involve working. Instead, my father invests money he doesn't have in schemes that are never going to work, and then expects me to pick up the bill when it all inevitably ends in disaster. Or when the roof starts caving in. Or any other time they're a little short, to be honest.'

'And do you? Pay, I mean?' Millie asked.

'I used to.'

Giles shifted his body further down the headboard, and turned them so they were facing each other, heads on pillows. It felt intimate, secret, in a way that went further than any of the passion they had shared.

'When I first started working I had dreams of using my salary to rebuild my family's fortunes. To save the legacy that looked so much in danger.'

'What changed?'

'It's more what *didn't* change,' Giles replied. 'My parents. They took the money happily enough, but they still wouldn't let me do anything new with the house or the land. They weren't willing to *do* anything except complain about the state of the house and ask for more money. And eventually…'

'You cut them off?'

'Yes.' Guilt hovered behind his eyes as he studied her face, obviously waiting for her reaction.

'I don't blame you,' she said easily. 'Helping

people is one thing. But you don't have to mortgage your own life for them.'

Even in the darkness of the bedroom she saw the surprise on his face before he kissed her. And she wondered how many times he'd been told he was selfish or ungrateful for making that choice. How much guilt he'd been made to feel.

She wished it was as simple as kissing that away.

Giles hadn't expected Millie to react the same way his parents and even his sister had to his decision to cut them off, but he hadn't dared to hope for such easy acceptance, either.

'They made you feel guilty about that, didn't they?' she asked, pulling away from the kiss.

'Yeah,' he admitted. 'They told me I was betraying the family name, our ancestors, the people who relied on our family and estate for work...everyone.'

And even though he *knew* that wasn't true—aside from anything else, he *did* still support a lot of the village and projects around the estate to provide employment for locals and such—it *felt* true.

'I'm sorry.' Millie ran a hand up his arm, warm comfort pouring out of her the way it always did. 'I still don't understand what any of this has to do with *you* getting married, though.'

He tried to find the words to explain.

'My parents' marriage was miserable—is *still* miserable and always will be. But my mum won't leave because the cachet of being Lady Fairfax is too great…even if the financial and everyday reality is so awful. Growing up watching them, I knew I could never put myself in a position like that. And then my sister Rebekah got married…'

He'd only been a teenager at the time, but he still remembered standing in the church, hoping against hope that someone would speak out when the vicar prompted anyone who knew of reasons why they shouldn't marry to do so.

Nobody had.

'That was even worse, somehow. She'd grown up in the same house I did—seen the same consequences I had every day—and yet she'd still… Her husband is not a good man. But he blinded her with charm and money and she believed herself passionately in love with him. Once they were married, he started to show his real character.'

'Why does she stay?' Millie asked.

Giles sighed. 'They have two kids—you helped me buy presents for them, remember? They're his heirs and she won't risk losing them. But it's not just that. She's told me flat that she's not willing to give up the lifestyle that her marriage affords her.'

And *that* was the part Giles didn't understand. When he'd been at school, he'd always been conscious of how precarious his own financial situation was compared to the other boys. Of what had been sold from the family estate to keep up appearances and send him there. He'd asked, once, if he couldn't go to the state school in the nearest town instead—and been so roundly rebuffed that he'd never asked again.

He hadn't understood then and he didn't now. Appearances didn't matter more than *reality*. Not to him, anyhow.

Millie snuggled a little closer and he felt her warmth against his bare skin. *This* was real. It might not be all it could be, and it certainly wasn't for ever, but right now he and Millie were real.

Even if her marriage wouldn't be.

Evidently her thoughts were running on similar lines, because she asked, 'Do you think I'm doing the same thing with Charlie?'

'Not entirely,' he said slowly. 'You genuinely do love and know each other, and your motives are less mercenary.'

'But apart from that…' She trailed off, and neither of them finished the sentence.

Because the truth was, yes. He did think it was the same thing, even with those caveats.

'So that's your parents and your sister,' Millie said, bringing the conversation back. 'What about you? Is it just their bad examples putting you off? Because I could counter that with plenty of better ones. My parents, for example.'

Giles shut his eyes. 'It's not just them. I mean…
a lot of it is. I don't want to carry on the family
tradition of being miserable in marriage just for
the look of the thing. And if I married and had
kids now, I'd owe it to *them* to save the house, the
estate. To give my parents all the money they ask
for. And that…'

It wasn't selfishness or greed that kept him
from paying them any more. It was the feeling
that to do so would be agreeing with them—that
the appearance mattered more than the truth, that
they deserved to sit around and have others pay
their way just by virtue of birth or marriage.

Maybe when they were gone and he could
sell the estate, or make it profitable somehow,
he would think again. But right now…

'You can't do that,' Millie said softly, and he
knew that somehow she understood. 'Not even
for true love.'

Her words caught him in the heart. And, although he hadn't meant to, he found himself telling her the *other* reason he would never marry.

'I thought once that maybe I could,' he admitted. 'There was a woman… Sienna. Back when
I'd just left university, and before I started making my own money. I loved her, and I thought
she loved me, and I was close to choosing a ring
when I overheard her in conversation with her
sister and realised that I was just a means to an

end for her. That she'd picked me to "fall in love with" because I met her criteria.'

Millie winced. 'Ouch. What did you do?'

'I told her about my family's financial troubles and watched her walk away.'

It had hurt at the time. It still did a little. But the lesson it had taught him was far more valuable to him than any relationship could be.

'So, marriage really is firmly off the cards for you,' Millie said. 'I can understand that.'

'Maybe one day that will change. But not while my parents are alive, I expect.'

It was a horrible admission to make. But Giles knew there was a worse one in his heart.

He was in love with Millie.

Despite all his best efforts to deny it, Giles at least tried to be honest with himself—to face reality instead of the illusion.

If he could marry anyone in this world it would be Millie. But he couldn't. Not when he couldn't give her everything she wanted—and not when it would destroy his own efforts to rebalance his family's impact on the world.

So instead he held her close, and didn't mention the fact that in just another few weeks she would be marrying someone else.

CHAPTER TWELVE

IT WAS TIME.

The past few months had been surreal—first planning her wedding with the best man rather than the groom, and then, for the last few weeks, falling into bed with him. But now the plan would get back on track. Her future was about to start.

Because Charlie had come home.

She and Giles had already agreed that the previous evening was to be their last night together. He hadn't even stayed overnight, for once, leaving just as the church bells chimed midnight.

She'd wrapped herself up in her duvet and walked him to the door of her flat, kissing him one last time—deep and hard—before she watched him walk away, down the stairs and through the shop, listening for the door locking behind him.

Then—and only then—had she cried.

She'd held the tears back during their final bout of lovemaking, even when Giles had held her closer than ever and whispered words she hadn't quite been able to hear against her skin. But as he'd left her for the last time she'd let them fall in acknowledgment of all they'd lost.

In another world, maybe there would have been a future for them. A future in which she could have let herself fall in love with him and hoped that he could love her, too. That they could be something more than great sex and incredible chemistry. More than the friends they were destined to be from now on.

But here and now she knew it couldn't work. She wanted marriage and a family *now*, while she still could—and that was something Giles absolutely would not and could not give her. It went against who he was in his soul. And since that was what she loved about him—

No. Not loved. Admired. Liked. Respected in a friend.

Definitely not love.

She wouldn't let herself love Giles that way when she knew she still didn't love Charlie as anything more than a friend. She didn't and couldn't want him the way she wanted Giles. Not when she still had to see him as a family friend for the rest of her life.

Millie hadn't slept much last night.

Eventually she'd got up in the pre-dawn darkness and sat with a cup of tea, preparing for the day ahead. In just a few hours Giles would be there to pick her up for the drive up to Norfolk together—as friends. She'd packed already, over the past couple of days, and her suitcase in the corner of her bedroom had been a constant reminder to both of them that their time was nearly up.

She needed the distraction of busyness, of wedding preparations—something to help her focus on the future ahead of her, not on what she'd had to give up. But everything all seemed to be done already.

Her dress had been sent ahead and was waiting for her at her mother's house. Her engagement ring was on her finger. Her hair and make-up would be done there by professionals, so she'd just packed her usual products. With the wedding being on Christmas Eve, they planned to stay and spend the festive season with their families before thinking about a honeymoon, or something similar, so she'd packed her every day clothes as well.

Would they be acceptable to wear when she was Charlie's wife? Well, if not, she was sure Tabby would take her shopping for more appropriate clothes.

What else?

She pulled up the packing checklist on her phone, squinting at the screen as she mentally checked off items.

Toothbrush, yes.

Toothpaste, yes.

Moisturiser, yes.

Tampons, yes.
Hairbrush, yes.
Wait.
Tampons…
She'd packed them, sure. But shouldn't she have needed them *before*?

Closing the checklist, she pulled up her cycle tracking app instead, realising immediately that she hadn't looked at it in a while. About five weeks, in fact.

Because she hadn't needed to track anything. She was late.

Almost five days late.

She blinked at the screen a few more times.

It could be wedding stress—it almost certainly *was* wedding stress, given her fertility issues and the fact that she and Giles had used protection. But still…

As she sat in the darkness, waiting for the man who was no longer her lover but the father of her hypothetical child to take her to her wedding to another man, Millie felt a tear slip down her cheek. The careful structure of lies and excuses she'd built over the last few weeks was starting to crack at last.

Millie was quiet on the drive up to Howard Hall. Subdued, even. Giles tried not to spend too much time looking at her instead of the road, but it was hard to shake the idea that there was something wrong.

Or maybe he was just projecting.

Saying goodbye to her the night before had been the hardest thing he'd ever done—right up until he'd come back this morning and tried to act normally around her. Friendly, but nothing more. No casual touches…no kiss pressed to the side of her head…no secret smiles that promised more later.

Just friends.

Yeah, *that* had been the hardest thing.

Or it had been until *now*, when he had to watch her in obvious distress, not knowing how much he was allowed to say or do to help her.

Maybe it was just the stress of the impending wedding getting to her. It was entirely possible—probable, even—that her low mood had nothing at all to do with him. She had a lot on her mind, after all.

That was what he told himself all the way along the long, straight road that led them into the depths of Norfolk.

Right up until the point when he saw the first tear roll down Millie's cheek.

He pulled over on the side of the road, killed the engine and unbuckled his seatbelt as he turned to her.

'What is it? What's the matter?'

There was panic in his voice; he could hear

it himself, as well as see it reflected in Millie's eyes. But she didn't answer.

'Is it the wedding? Have you changed your mind?' he pressed. 'Because, Millie, I swear to God if you want out I will get you out. I'll turn the car around now, take you home, then come back and sort everything. I'll be the bad guy. Whatever you need, I can do it.'

He wasn't even sure himself what he wanted her answer to be. It wasn't as if he was asking her to choose him over Charlie. He wasn't an option—he couldn't give her the life she wanted. He wanted her to be happy. That was all.

But whatever answer he expected from her, it wasn't the one he got.

'I'm late.'

He blinked, trying to process the two tiny words. And as they finally swirled into making sense in his head, the world around them seemed to stop cold.

'You're *pregnant*?'

He wished he hadn't sounded quite so incredulous. But they'd been careful. And wasn't the whole point of her getting married to Charlie the fact that she probably *couldn't* get pregnant easily?

'Almost certainly not,' Millie admitted. 'But… there's a chance. And I can't marry Charlie tomorrow if I'm pregnant with your baby, can I? So I have to…check. But the pharmacy in the village opened late today, so I couldn't get a test, and now I'll have to find somewhere to get one when we get to Howard Hall, and I—'

Giles grabbed her hands, holding them to his chest, very aware that it was the first time he'd touched her since they'd said goodbye the night before.

'There's a town at the next junction. I'll pull off there and get you a test. We'll stop at a café or something for some proper breakfast and you can take it. *Then* we'll talk about what happens next—okay?'

She nodded mutely.

Giles knew he should leave it there, but everything inside him told him that he couldn't.

So he pressed a small kiss to her knuckles and murmured, 'It's going to be okay, sweetheart. One way or another. I promise.'

It wasn't a promise that was really his to give. He knew that. But he couldn't stop himself. He wanted to make things right for her—to take responsibility. After all, if she *was* pregnant it was at least half his doing.

Exactly *how* he'd make it right... Well, he didn't know yet. But for the first time since he'd left her flat the night before the tightness that had taken up residence in his chest started to loosen and he could breathe again.

That had to mean something, didn't it?

* * *

The test was negative.

That shouldn't have been a surprise—Millie knew how low her chances of conceiving naturally were. And yet…she *was* surprised.

When she'd realised her period was late, she'd sort of assumed it must be a sign from the universe, telling her to take a different path. But apparently the universe wasn't watching. Or it was, and it was rooting for her and Charlie.

Which was what she should be doing, too.

Giles certainly was. She'd never seen a man so relieved by a negative pregnancy test. Well, she didn't actually have any other men or tests to compare it to, but still… He'd been pretty damn relieved.

'Let's go and get you married, then,' he'd said, smiling.

And off they'd driven to Howard Hall, leaving the remains of their breakfast and a generous tip behind on the café table.

And now here they were…sitting in his car in the driveway of Howard Hall, about to head in.

'You're ready?' Giles asked, not looking at her.

'As I'll ever be,' she responded.

Not the most ringing endorsement of a wedding ever, she supposed. But honest, at least.

'Then let's go.'

She risked one last glance at him and thought, just for a second, that she saw a hint of the same pain she felt in his eyes. But it was gone in a flash and there was Charlie—safe, wonderful, loyal Charlie—waiting for her on the stairs.

Millie pushed down any last, lingering thoughts about what might have been and walked towards him, only half hearing Giles behind her, saying that he'd see them at the rehearsal dinner.

'Everything okay?' Charlie murmured as they hugged.

'It's all going to be fine now,' Millie replied.

And she almost believed it.

Up until the point when Charlie left her alone in what was apparently going to be her new rooms and she burst into tears for everything that might have been and never could be.

Giles resisted the urge to go and get blind drunk—but only just.

He also resisted the urges that followed, like dominos in a line. First, to go and find Millie and tell her that he was wrong, that he loved her, that she shouldn't marry Charlie and instead they should just carry on exactly the way they'd been, except she'd get none of the future she wanted, but he'd be happy so that was fine, wasn't it?

The other urge was even less useful—the desire to head down to the gatehouse and bare his soul to Millie's mother. He'd only met the woman once, but he already knew she'd be more sympathetic and helpful than his own parents.

But Millie didn't want her mum to know she wasn't marrying for true love, so that option was out, too.

As a last resort, he went for a walk around the extensive Howard Hall gardens—despite the fact that all the flowers were dead because it was winter—and tried to make sense of the rollercoaster of emotions he'd experienced that day.

First, there had been the pain of leaving Millie, knowing he'd never hold her, have her the way he had again. That had hurt maybe more than he'd expected, but he'd at least expected it.

The pregnancy scare had come out of nowhere.

Could he even call it a scare, when he'd only known about it for an hour before they saw that negative test? Millie must have sat with it for longer, and a pregnancy was a longed-for thing for her. Even if he wasn't the ideal father, given the circumstances, she must have wanted it at least a little bit.

And he…he didn't. He *didn't.* He didn't want to have to explain to his best friend how he'd got his fiancée pregnant. He didn't want to put Millie in that position either. He didn't want to have to row back on all his years of campaigning to use his family estate for the wider good, to end the entitlement of his ancestors instead of just blindly handing it on to the next generation. He didn't want to tie himself into a family he didn't want just because of one mistake. That would surely be the worst thing he could do to Millie and any child—to make them both miserable for ever just because of a failure of contraception. Just like his parents had done.

He would have done it, though, he realised. If she'd been pregnant, and if what she'd wanted was marriage, he would have done it. For her. Because he loved her and he couldn't bear to hurt her any more than he already had done.

But she didn't love him. And even if she grew to love him it was hardly an auspicious start, was it? If they were forced to marry under those circumstances, it would only increase their chances of resentment and bitterness in the future, leading down that inevitable path to a marriage like his parents', or his sister's. One that would poison every beautiful moment he and Millie had ever shared.

He couldn't have taken that. So he was glad she wasn't pregnant.

Except…

He wouldn't admit it to anyone else—hell, he could barely admit it to himself—but for a brief, fleeting second when he'd heard the words 'I'm late' he'd pictured it. Millie, round with his baby, beaming up at him—not in a wedding dress, but *his* all the same.

And for that brief, fleeting, blink-and-you'd-miss-it second, he'd *wanted* it.

But it wasn't his to want. He'd known that when

they'd started their fling, and he couldn't forget it now. Millie had chosen the life she wanted, and it wasn't the life he wanted. And she'd chosen it for Charlie's sake as much as for herself—for a man who was the closest thing he'd ever have to a brother.

He wouldn't ruin that for either of them.

That future wasn't in the cards for him, and that was a *good* thing.

He just had to keep reminding himself of that.

Grimly determined to do just that, Giles stomped back inside Howard Hall to the room he'd been assigned to get ready for the wedding rehearsal and associated dinner that night.

Not for me. Not for me.

Chanting the words in his head seemed to help as he watched Millie, smiling and practically glowing with happiness, beside Charlie at the top of the table. The rehearsal dinner was being held in the formal dining room of Howard Hall—a space too small for tomorrow's wedding breakfast, but still vast enough to host everyone staying at the house the night before the wedding.

Just an hour or so before he'd stood beside Charlie in the tiny family chapel on the estate as they'd rehearsed their lines for the following day. He'd listened carefully and nodded when the vicar had told him at which point he'd hand over the rings, and pushed away the memory of sliding Millie's engagement ring onto her finger. He hadn't been able to stop himself looking away when Charlie had bent his head to place a chaste kiss against Millie's lips, on the vicar's orders.

It was good that there had been a rehearsal, he told himself now, as he pushed a piece of chicken around his plate. He'd needed the practice. To rehearse smiling and looking happy as Charlie and Millie pledged their troth to each other. To manage to make polite conversation with his table neighbours even as he felt his heart was cracking in two.

He'd made it through the rehearsal. He'd make it through the real thing, too.

As they finished up their desserts Millie got to her feet, and Giles braced himself all over again. He'd helped her pick out the dress she was wearing tonight—a deep, emerald-green silk that swept across her curves elegantly. The perfect dress for the future lady of the manor.

She tapped a fork against the side of her glass and the room fell silent. On either side of her, Charlie and her mum were beaming up at her—approving, happy and loving. With a smile, she started to speak—confident and clear, and with no sign at all of the stressful morning she'd had, thanks to him.

He should never have started anything with her. He'd known it was wrong at the time, for all that they apparently had Charlie's blessing. It was wrong to start something he couldn't finish. Millie wasn't the sort of woman he could mess around with.

He should have known he'd end up with a broken heart.

He was only half listening to her speech—thanking her fiancé and family and such—until he heard his own name.

'Finally, I want to say a special thank-you to Charlie's best friend and best man, Giles. When Charlie's work dragged him away, Giles stepped up and helped me organise all sorts of wedding-related things—from invitations to flowers and rings. And I can tell you he can now put together a pretty impressive festive wreath, too!'

That got a laugh, and he didn't even mind that it was at his expense.

'Seriously, though. Thank you, Giles, for everything.'

She looked right at him as she said it, and he raised his glass to toast her in response. When she sat down again, he knew it was really, truly over. His part in her life was over.

She had her dream, and she was marrying the man who could give it to her.

Just like he'd told her to.

CHAPTER THIRTEEN

THE REHEARSAL DINNER was over. All the guests
had retired to their rooms, to rest up for the day
ahead tomorrow. Millie had told her mum she
didn't need her to stay with her, and she'd even
managed to send Tabby away, too. She was alone.
And she was too nervous to rest.

But she had a feeling that someone else—just
one person in the world—would be feeling the
same tonight.

Slipping out through the back door of Howard
Hall without being seen was tricky—the huge
house seemed to be full of people preparing for
the wedding—but she managed it...just. With her
big coat wrapped over her pyjamas, and her feet
in thick socks under someone else's wellies that
she'd found in the boot room, she sneaked outside
and shut the door silently behind her.

The night was dark, lit only by the pale lights
from the windows of Howard Hall, but Millie
knew her path well. Once she was out of sight
of the house she pulled out her phone to use the

torch, tramping through the woods behind the gardens until the stone walls of the ruined folly came into view.

She smiled as another figure stood as she approached, a bottle of champagne in his hand.

'Millie?'

'Who else?' She took the last few steps and dropped to sit on the wall beside Charlie. 'Did you bring a second glass for me?'

'I didn't even bring one for me.'

Charlie took a gulp from the neck of the bottle, then handed it over to Millie, who copied the movement before passing it back.

'I wasn't really expecting company.'

'Why not?' Millie tucked her feet up onto the wall so her knees were her under her chin, her arms wrapped around them. 'We always used to meet here as kids. And teens, for that matter.'

'Yeah, but…everything's different now, isn't it?'

'I suppose.' It *felt* different, that was for sure. 'But if we're really getting married tomorrow I don't *want* it to be different. I want it to be like it always was between us. Don't you?'

'*If* we're getting married?' Charlie raised his eyebrows at her. 'Having doubts?'

'No,' she said quickly. 'Why? Are you?'

'Of course not.'

They sat in silence for a moment. Then Charlie said, 'So… Giles. He really was a help? I know you two haven't always got on so well, and I really did feel bad about having to go away and leave it all to you two, but—'

'No. He was great. He... I couldn't have done it all without him.'

'Good.' Charlie gave her a speculative look. 'Only...the way he was watching you at the dinner, I wondered if maybe something had happened between you two?'

Groaning, Millie sank her forehead to her knees. 'Were we that obvious?'

'You weren't,' Charlie replied. 'But he was. To me, anyway.'

'I'm sorry. We didn't mean for it to happen. It was just—'

What? Convenient? Inevitable because they were spending time together? A last fling before the ring, just as she'd said it would be?

But Millie knew in her heart it wasn't any of those things. Not by the end.

She loved him. But that didn't matter because he didn't want the things she did, and he was too damn stubborn to give up on what *he* wanted either.

'It's fine.' Charlie brushed away her apologies. 'We both agreed that if we wanted to have a last few weeks of freedom we should. And at least it was with Giles. I don't have to worry about his stealing you away and marrying you before I can!'

'Right...' She stole a glance across at her fiancé. 'What about you? Did you find someone to…to sow those last wild oats with in Scotland, while you were away?'

Even in the moonlight she could see the dark red flush flooding his cheeks.

Grinning, she shifted to face him. 'You did! Who was she?'

Charlie looked awkward, and his words sounded strangely formal as he explained about his unexpected, unintended Scottish fling.

'But it's done now,' he finished, his expression suddenly sobering. 'And I'm here. I'm committed to you, Mills. I won't let you down. I promise.'

'I know.'

Octavia had been Charlie's one true love and, if Millie was honest, she was beginning to suspect that maybe Giles had been hers. But if neither of them could have that heartbreaking, frustrating version of love, at least they could have *this*. Marrying her best friend wasn't a second choice—it was a sensible one. And she knew he needed it as much as she did. She wouldn't let him down either.

She reached for the bottle and toasted him with it. 'To us,' she said, before drinking.

With a soft smile, Charlie took it back and drank, too. 'To us.'

Giles had important best man duties to be doing this morning—he knew that. But the wedding wasn't until the afternoon, and it wasn't as if he'd slept much after the rehearsal dinner, anyway. So, very early on Christmas Eve, he crept away from Howard Hall and drove to his sister Rebekah's house to play Santa.

After all, he wouldn't want the gifts he and Millie had chosen so carefully to get forgotten. And seeing them sitting in the corner of his room was only reminding him of the time they'd spent together, anyway.

Rebekah was surprised to see him, that much was obvious, but she ushered him in anyway. The kids, clearly already in a Christmas Eve frenzy of excitement, came thundering down the main staircase, narrowly avoiding dislodging the carefully wound garland on the banister and crashing into the eight-foot colour-coordinated tree at the bottom.

'Uncle Giles!' his niece cried, with a gratifying amount of excitement in her voice.

'Have you brought us presents?' her younger brother asked, with the same excitement but more mercenary meaning.

He laughed. 'As it happens, I have.'

'Let's go through and have coffee while they open them,' Rebekah suggested.

Settled in Rebekah's meticulously designed and decorated morning room—a family space off the modern kitchen in a glass extension at the back of the much older house that looked out

SOPHIE PEMBROKE   227

over the extensive gardens beyond—he let his
sister pour them both strong, black coffees as
they watched the kids rip the paper off their gifts.

'Unexpectedly thoughtful this year,' Rebekah
said, not unkindly. 'New girlfriend?'

The kids hugged him in thanks, then both ran
off to play with their early presents.

Rebekah, however, was still waiting for an answer.

'Not exactly,' he hedged. 'I did have a friend
to help me shop…'

'A friend?' The disbelief in his sister's voice
was palpable.

'It's complicated.'

'Isn't it always?'

Not this *complicated*, he thought, but didn't
say.

How could he possibly explain that he was
playing best man at the wedding of the woman
he loved later that day?

'Marc not here?' he asked, in an attempt to
change the subject.

Rebekah shook her head. 'Working in London, so he stayed at the flat there last night—
well, the last few nights. He'll be back in time
to see the kids open their stockings in the morning, I'm sure.

'Right.'

Giles didn't comment. He had a million things
he *wanted* to say, but he'd said them all to his

sister before and it had only driven them further apart. Today, of all days, he couldn't face another fight.

But she gave him a sideways look all the same. 'I know what you're thinking.'

'I didn't say anything.'

'You didn't have to.' She sighed. 'I know you don't understand it, Gilly. Honestly, some days I don't either. But I made my bed and I'm damned if I'll let anyone else lie in it. Like you said, love—marriage—is complicated. But when you get right down to it I love my kids more than the world, so I will stay here in this house and get to be with them every single day.'

'And when they're grown up?'

This was the closest she'd ever come to admitting that she might be unhappy in her marriage. And, while he didn't necessarily agree with her logic, he couldn't exactly refute it either.

'Then we'll see,' she said simply.

They sat in silence for a long moment, Rebekah swirling her coffee around in her cup.

Then, out of nowhere, she said, 'I had another choice, you know. Another love, I mean. Stronger, even. It came too late, of course—I was already engaged. Still, I know it could have been... But it would have meant giving up *everything*. Marc had the money, the social standing—we were invited everywhere as a couple...we *mattered*. Paul... He had none of that, and no hope of getting it either. I'd have been ostracised by friends and family for leaving Marc, too. And, like I said, this was years ago. When things were good with Marc. When I still had hope for what my marriage could be...the life we might live together. And so I let it pass by. I just... I didn't realise how much of myself I'd lose, married to Marc instead.'

Giles reached over and grabbed her hands, gripping them tight. 'You know that if you are ever ready to leave I will get you out. No questions, no fuss. You just call.'

'I know.' She gave him a watery smile. 'Maybe one day. But not yet.'

He studied her face for another long moment, then nodded, releasing her hands. She hadn't given up yet, even if he couldn't see from the outside what she was fighting for. The life she'd built, the future she expected, he supposed. It was hard to give up those dreams, those convictions.

He knew that, didn't he? His convictions might be the opposite of hers, but they were every bit as strongly held.

Still, when he left he was still picturing his sister's face, and praying that Millie and Charlie wouldn't be having the same regrets in ten years' time.

Millie hadn't wanted a whole party of bridesmaids to troop after her down the tiny aisle of the family chapel, all dressed in identical dresses with matching hairstyles. She'd debated long and hard about who to ask, but in the end she'd kept it simple. Tabby would stand up with her as her adult bridesmaid, and they'd pop pretty velvet party dresses on her cousin's two small daughters and call it good.

But despite the bridesmaid streamlining it still felt as if the world and his wife were in her suite at Howard Hall on this, the morning of the wedding. What with her mum, Tabby, her cousin supervising her daughters *and* the hair stylist and make-up artist, it was getting a little crowded.

Millie gravitated towards the window, staring out at the frosty wonderland of the Howard Hall gardens outside, wondering if she could open one of the sash windows and suck in a lungful or two of crisp, fresh air.

'This is the suite we always provide for brides at Howard Hall.' Tabby eyed the space critically. 'Maybe we need to put some more mirrors in here for them.'

'I'm sure that would help,' Millie replied, thinking of how hundreds more reflections of people would actually make her feel even more trapped.

Tabby gave her a sharp look. 'Are you okay?'

Millie swallowed. 'Fine. Just a bit…overwhelmed.'

'Of course.'

With an understanding smile and a few soft words somehow Tabby managed to herd everyone out of the room—well, everyone except Millie's mum, which was just right.

'*Are* you okay, sweetheart?' Jessica Myles wrapped an arm around Millie's shoulders where she stood at the window, being careful not to crease the beautiful wedding dress they'd chosen together.

'I'm fine,' Millie replied quickly.

But it was a lie, and from the way her mum hesitated and watched her, she knew it, too.

With a last squeeze of her shoulder, Jessica stepped away from her side, only to lean against the windowsill in front of her. Millie met her gaze, then looked away again—fast. The gleam in her mother's eye was all too knowing, as if it saw right into her heart. There were things in there she definitely didn't want her mum to see— especially today.

But all Jessica said was, 'You look so beautiful, sweetheart. The dress is perfect, and so are you. Charlie is going to be blown away.' There was a catch in her voice, and then… 'Your dad would be so proud of you, you know. Oh, not just for this—not for marrying a Howard. For who you are and everything you've done. The wonderful woman you've grown into.'

Tears pricked behind Millie's eyes. 'I hope so.'

'I *know* so.' Jessica reached out and ran a palm

down Millie's arm. 'I wish, more than anything, that he was here today to see you…to walk you down the aisle.'

'So do I,' Millie admitted. 'But… I'm glad that *you* get to do that, too.'

Jessica nodded. 'One thing I do know… If he was here, he'd want to ask you one last time. Are you sure about this? About marrying Charlie? Because it's still not too late—'

'Why wouldn't I be sure?' Millie tried for a confident smile. 'I'm marrying my best friend—just like you did when you married Dad. Isn't that what you always said I should look for in a husband? Someone who was my best friend, like Dad was for you?'

'Yes. I did say that.' Jessica looked away, out of the window, perhaps hoping that if she looked hard enough she might even see her late husband out there amongst the frosty greenery. 'And it still holds. But Millie…that wasn't *all* he was. Friendship matters, but in a marriage you need a partner. Someone who will always be there for you—be fundamentally on your side even when you disagree about the details. Someone you can trust to always come through for you.'

'Charlie has always come through for me.'

Except the part where he ran off to Scotland and left her to organise their wedding.

'Charlie has been a very, very good friend to you,' Jessica agreed. 'But I wasn't finished. Trust

runs deeper than just friendship. You need someone you can trust with your *passion*. With your
body...your soul. You need someone you can con-
nect with on a physical level.'

Millie looked away. This was *not* the sort of
conversation she usually had with her mother.

But Jessica grabbed her hands. 'I *know* we
don't talk about these things—I always trusted
that you had your female friends to talk about
sex and such with, beyond the essential basics of
consent and safety. But, Millie, this *matters*. Yes,
I told you to marry someone who could be your
best friend—but I'd be doing you a disservice if
I told you that was all there was to it. Marriage
is more than friendship. It's passion. It's *love*—
bone-deep and part of your soul. The part that
connects you when you make love, make *life*.
And if Charlie isn't that for you—if you're not
that for *him*—and if there's someone else who
could be—'

She broke off as Millie looked up to meet her
gaze.

'How did you know?' Millie asked in a whisper.

Jessica smiled. 'I saw you two together, remember?'

That had been long before anything had ever
happened between her and Giles, but apparently
it didn't matter. It had still been there between
them...waiting.

It still was, even though they'd said goodbye. She was starting to think it always would be.

Millie swallowed. 'I need to talk to Charlie. I need to talk to—'

'Giles,' her mum finished for her.

And Millie nodded, suddenly ashamed of letting things get this far, and yet at the same time knowing it didn't really change anything.

Because she wasn't willing to give up her dream of a family, and she knew that Giles didn't want that. But she wasn't willing to settle for anything less than she'd found with Giles now she knew it was possible. Maybe it wouldn't be with him, but if she'd found it once she could find it again—couldn't she?

She'd freeze her eggs. She'd look into adoption—or fostering, even. She'd take her chances and design her own life, full of passion and love and friendship.

But she couldn't marry Charlie.

CHAPTER FOURTEEN

CHARLIE'S HANDS WERE SHAKING. And Giles was pretty sure the groom hadn't had a drink that morning, or even much the night before, so he assumed it had to be nerves. Stress, even.

It was getting hard to pretend he didn't know why.

Charlie gripped hold of the windowsill in front of him, his knuckles white as he stared out at the driveway and the approach to Howard Hall, watching the guests arrive, and Giles knew he had to say something.

'Charlie… Millie told me about why the two of you decided to get married so fast.'

His best friend looked back at him over his shoulder. 'The way she tells it, that's not the only thing the two of you shared while I was away.'

Giles looked away. 'I didn't know she… She said that you told her to have a last fling, if she wanted.'

Charlie's laugh was hollow. 'I did, God help

me. I thought it would help us both reconcile ourselves to marriage.'

Which Giles took to mean that Millie wasn't the only one to take advantage of that agreement. He wondered who Charlie had found up in Scotland.

It didn't matter now, though. What mattered was Charlie and Millie and whether they should get married at all. Because from the grey sheen on Charlie's face, he was having second thoughts.

It'll break Millie if he doesn't go through with it.

Giles frowned at the thought. Would it? Would it, really?

Millie was stronger than that. Stronger than he'd ever given her credit for. And probably stronger than even Charlie knew.

If that test hadn't been negative Giles had no doubt that Millie would have walked in here, owned up to everything, called off the wedding and then gone out and been the most kick-ass single mum in the world if he hadn't been willing to stand with her.

Except he would have been. He'd have been right there at her side if she'd needed him. But that wasn't the way the dice had fallen.

Still…

'If you're having second thoughts about this wedding, you need to tell Millie,' Giles told his friend.

Because walking away on their wedding day would hurt Millie, for sure. But marrying her and making them both miserable because it wasn't what he really wanted…? That would be the one thing that *would* destroy her.

He couldn't watch Millie and Charlie end up like his sister and her husband. He loved them *both* too much for that.

'I'm *not* having second thoughts,' Charlie snapped back, too vehemently for Giles to believe him.

He spun round to face Giles, his hand no longer shaking as he spoke, emphasising his points with a pointing finger.

'Millie is one of the best people I know, and I love her. She needs this, and I'd never let her down like that. She wants a family, a happy-ever-after, and if no one else is going to give it to her then I'm damn well going to make sure she gets it—because she deserves *everything.*'

'I know,' Giles said quietly. Because she really did.

And he'd give anything to be the one to give it to her.

Anything? his mind asked.

Would he give up his preconceived ideas about marriage? His beliefs about the right thing to do with his family legacy? His bitter revenge against his parents?

Because that was what it would take, right?

Charlie's eyes narrowed as he watched him. 'And what about you, Giles? So quick with the advice for others, but what do *you* want? I thought it really was just a fling before the ring between you and Millie, like we agreed. But looking at you now, I'm not so sure.'

Giles felt the blood drain from his face. 'I'll stay away once you're married, Charlie. You know I'd never betray you that way. Millie and I ended everything before we came here. You know I can't give her what she wants.'

'But you wish you could, don't you?'

Charlie's words hit too close to his own thoughts, and Giles stepped back, turning away to fuss with the tray of buttonholes Millie had sent up.

White roses with dark green sprigs of leaves. Just like they'd planned.

Oh, God, he'd helped plan this entire day, and in the process he'd almost forgotten it wasn't his wedding.

'You're here asking what *I* want, but have you thought about what *you* want?' Charlie took a step closer, into Giles's space, forcing him to look up at him. 'Or have you spent so long focussing on what you *don't* want—on *not* falling in love, *not* getting married, *not* ending up like your parents or your sister, or chained to a money pit of a house because of history and society and expectations—that you've forgotten to even *think* about what *you* want?'

The words hit home, and they hit deep.

Because there was a moment when he'd let those thoughts of what *he* wanted in.

When he'd thought Millie might be carrying his child and against the odds…against everything he'd thought he believed in, every conviction he had…he'd wanted it. He'd wanted Millie and their child and that damn happy-ever-after that he hadn't even *believed* in until he'd fallen in love with her. Maybe not right now—he wasn't fool enough to think that he could overturn his whole belief system and understanding of the world overnight. But someday.

And for ever.

God, he'd *never* thought he'd want for ever.

He turned to Charlie, knowing his mouth was gaping open and unsure what to do about it. He had no words.

Charlie had been his best friend for most of his life. He'd helped form him into the person he was—helped him see that there was another way to live in the world than the one his parents had chosen. That he could live a life of contribution and creation rather than entitlement and acceptance. He'd helped him become a man he was proud to be.

A man who could fall more deeply in love than he'd ever imagined, as it turned out.

Charlie was his best friend and he'd betrayed him. And yet somehow he was still smiling.

'So. When exactly did you fall in love with my fiancée?' Charlie asked. 'And just what are you going to do about it?'

Millie raced down the stairs of Howard Hall, hoping she was early enough to catch Charlie before he headed to the chapel and to avoid the guests arriving early for a welcome drink before the service.

She recoiled as she hit a wall of sound—people in hats and fancy outfits were everywhere, and the levels of gossip and chatter were epic. She spotted Tabby in her bridesmaid's dress, ushering people into one of the many reception rooms, but she couldn't see the best man anywhere.

She did see her groom.

Charlie waded through the crowd, against the tide of people heading in the opposite direction, and grabbed hold of the bottom of the banister. 'Want to get out of here for a moment?'

Millie nodded enthusiastically, and before she knew it he'd whisked her back up the stairs and into a tiny side room—or was it a cupboard?—she'd never noticed before, halfway up the staircase. There were racks of fur coats against one wall, and for a moment Millie wondered if Charlie was suggesting they run away to Narnia.

It didn't sound like such a bad idea right now.

Except, given her outfit—and what she was about to do—she'd probably be cast as the White Witch.

'You aren't supposed to see me in my wedding dress before the ceremony,' she said, looking down at her wide white skirts, and seeing only Giles's face when he'd walked into the dress shop.

'I think that only counts if the wedding is actually going to take place.'

Charlie's voice was soft—kind, even—and when she looked up at him there was no anger in his face. If anything, she thought she saw…relief.

'Is it?' he asked.

'I… I don't think it can. I'm sorry, Charlie. I can't marry you.'

Just saying the words lifted a weight from her shoulders that she knew, if she'd gone through with the wedding, would have broken her down eventually. Walking away from Charlie was hard. But not as impossible as it would have been to be married to him, knowing she was in love with someone else.

'Because you're in love with Giles.'

It wasn't a question, more a statement of fact. And, actually…was Charlie *smiling*?

'You're not…angry?'

Millie knew others would be. Everyone who'd come all this way on Christmas Eve. And Tabby had put all that into the wedding. Not to mention the money…

But Charlie shook his head. 'I'm not angry.

I'm… Honestly, right at this moment, I'm not sure what I am. Except your best friend. I'll always be that.'

She smiled up at him, reaching out to grip his hand tight, trying to convey all the love and gratitude she had for him and his place in her life in just that gesture.

She loved him—deeply. But, looking up at him now, she didn't know how she'd ever believed she could be his wife.

'How did we end up here?' Millie asked. 'I mean…really?'

Charlie shrugged helplessly, then wrapped his arms around her and pulled her into a hug. 'I think we both wanted to make each other happy. And maybe we would have done. But it would only ever have been a sort of…'

'Contentment.' Millie finished for him when he trailed off. 'We'd have been content, I think. Except now we both know there's something more out there, and it's hard to settle for contentment after that.'

'It is.' Charlie placed a kiss to the top of her head, then stepped away. 'So I think we'd both better get out there and demand what we *really* want from life. Don't you?'

Millie slipped out of the closet, surprised to find the hall below already empty. Where had everybody gone? Then she spotted the grandfather clock. It was time for the ceremony.

They'd all gone to the chapel.

Leaving Charlie behind—he'd offered to go with her, but she'd insisted she be the one to do it—she padded down the stairs, hiking up her wedding dress so she didn't trip over it, and ran out through the front door towards the family chapel.

Frost crunched underfoot as she ran across the grass. The chapel wasn't far, but she shivered as the cold air hit her bare arms all the same. As she approached, she could see her mum and Tabby waiting just outside, and she saw the panic on Tabby's face. Of course. Charlie wasn't there. And his sister wouldn't want to have to break the news to his bride.

She tried to smile to reassure them, but then she heard a voice—one that her heart recognised as well as her ears.

'Don't worry,' she murmured to Tabby and her mum as she continued towards the voice. 'I've got this part covered. But there is something I need you to do, Tabby.'

She filled Charlie's sister in on what they needed from her as quickly as she could. Now she'd started on this path she was impatient to reach its end.

'But—' Tabby started, but Jessica placed a hand on her arm and nodded to Millie.

244   CHRISTMAS BRIDE'S STAND-IN GROOM

'You go on, love,' her mum said.

And Millie paused just long enough to place a kiss on her cheek and whisper, 'Thanks, Mum.'

The heavy wooden door of the chapel opened easily under her hands and swung closed behind her, Tabby and Jessica having slipped inside in her wake. Millie ignored the crowds of people and focussed on Giles, standing by the altar, trying to reassure people.

'If you could all be patient for just a few more moments...' Giles was saying, as the door banged shut.

The chapel fell silent as all the guests turned to watch Millie walk down the aisle. At the front, the string quartet started playing her processional music—until Tabby appeared from the side of the chapel to shush them.

But Millie kept her gaze on Giles, who stared right back. One hand darted out to indicate the empty space beside him, where Charlie should be standing, but Millie merely smiled serenely.

Everything was going to be fine. Oh, maybe not immediately—she was pretty sure that untangling this mess was going to take some work. But she knew Charlie would probably face the worst of it, having to explain everything to his parents and all their friends.

The only people here whose opinion Millie really cared about were on her side—her mum,

Charlie and, she hoped, Giles. Even Tabby would come round eventually, she was sure.

Everything was going to be all right now.

No, better than all right.

She was going to make her future *glorious*.

Millie reached the front of the chapel. Giles stepped aside with a confused look on his face. Then she turned to face the crowd and began to speak.

CHAPTER FIFTEEN

GILES HAD NO idea what was happening.

He knew that Charlie was having doubts about the wedding, and hoped that his friend had gone to talk to Millie about it while Giles stalled at the chapel. But now here was Millie, walking down the aisle alone to where Giles stood, without her groom beside him.

Had Charlie found her?

Had they talked?

What was she feeling right now?

Whatever it was, it didn't look as if it was clenching at her heart the way his own anxiety and concern and hope were his.

Millie smiled beatifically out at the crowd of gawping congregants, clasped her hands in front of her, where her bouquet should be, and began to talk.

'Thank you all so much for coming out on such a cold and frosty morning to support Charlie and I today. Unfortunately, I have to tell you that there won't be a wedding today. Charlie and

I have decided that, much as we love and adore each other as best friends, and always will, that friendship isn't enough to sustain decades of marriage together.'

A murmur was going around the crowd now. Giles wondered where Charlie was…whether Millie had asked him to let her do this. He thought she probably had. He wouldn't have left her alone otherwise.

Except he hadn't left her alone, had he? Charlie would have known that Giles would be here, standing right beside her.

Maybe that was why he wasn't there. He was giving Giles his chance to stand up and do the right thing.

And finally Giles thought he might even know what that was.

'But, while there isn't a wedding today, it *is* still Christmas Eve, and I know the Howard family are still excited to celebrate the season with you all up at the house. After all, life, love and friendship should *always* be celebrated, don't you think?'

At a look from Millie, the string quartet burst into action again, playing a rousing chorus of 'We Wish You a Merry Christmas', while Tabby and Jessica opened the chapel doors wide and began ushering guests back to the hall. A few stopped to offer their condolences to Millie as they passed, but every time she shook her head and told them that this was the best for everyone, and she'd rather keep Charlie as her best friend than her future ex-husband—a line that got at least a few polite laughs.

Giles suspected they all thought she was just putting on a brave face. But he knew her better than that, and knew she was telling the truth.

More than that, she was glowing. With happiness, or anticipation, or hope—or something else he couldn't even identify but hoped she'd explain.

Then, as the last guest left the chapel and the door closed behind them, she turned to him—with all that hope and happiness on full, glowing display—and smiled.

And Giles's heart began to soar.

Telling a crowd of society's finest, who'd traipsed out to Norfolk on Christmas Eve to see a society wedding, that there wasn't going to *be* a wedding was easy.

Telling the man left behind that it was because she was in love with him was going to be much harder.

Or so she thought.

Millie turned to find Giles watching her cautiously, a very small smile dancing around his lips.

'You changed your mind, then?' he asked.

'We both did, I think,' Millie replied. 'But mostly it didn't seem right for me to marry Charlie when I was in love with someone else.'

The slight, sharp intake of breath she heard was probably because of the cold. He *had* to know she loved him by now, didn't he?

'Millie, I—'

She knew what he was going to say, so she cut him off before he could start.

'Giles, look... I know we agreed that this would only ever be a fling. That you hate the idea of marriage and children and all that. I can understand why—even if I don't agree with you—but I'm in love with you anyway. I'm in love with the way you look at me, the way you touch me, the way you think of me and care for me. It makes me want to do the same for you. You've taught me what I want from love. And even if you can't ever give it to me, I'm not willing to settle for anything less now I know what love can be.'

She stared at him with defiant, wide eyes and waited for his response. Because this was it. This was the moment when she knew which way her future would go.

But Giles didn't say anything. Instead, he lurched forward and wrapped her into his arms, kissing her hard and deep.

As answers went, Millie had definitely been predicting worse. But just as she was settling into the kiss he pulled back again, resting his forehead against hers as he stared into her eyes. His arms were still tight around her waist, and Millie felt as if he might never, ever let her go.

And she was fine with that.

'You know I love you, too, don't you?' His words were harsh, desperate. 'You have to know that?'

'I... I hoped,' Millie replied. 'I wouldn't say *knew*. And I definitely didn't think you'd admit it.'

His eyes fluttered closed as he gave her a rueful smile. 'I know. I... Love, commitment, marriage—it all felt like a trap to me. Just another angle on the legacy and expectation my parents placed on me from birth, because of the title and the crumbling estate and everything that was coming to me when my father dies. It was as if, if I ever fell in love and married, they'd have me at last. Because of course I'd have to save the estate for my wife and kids. I was scared... Not of the work, but of becoming like them. Of turning into what they've become. Hating each other but never able to leave. I couldn't—'

'I know,' Millie whispered. 'I understand.'

'I don't think you do,' he said. 'Because the thing I've realised is...you'd never let that happen. *You're* not like them. You're...magical, Millie, to me. The way you see the world, the way you live in it... You'd never be like them, and so *I* would never be like them. When you told me you might be pregnant... I think my heart stopped, just for a moment. And I realised afterwards that it wasn't fear that did that. It was longing. I *wanted* that life with you. I wanted any reason at all to stop you marrying Charlie and choose me instead. I wanted an excuse to put all my old beliefs behind me, and I thought that might be it.'

'You…want that?'

Millie fought back the hopeful feeling swelling inside her—just in case. She needed to hear him say it. Not just that he'd have taken the excuse if it presented itself—he needed to *want* it.

'With me?'

'I want…'

Giles looked up at the ceiling of the chapel and she watched his Adam's apple bob as he swallowed.

'Millie. I love you. I want you in my life for ever. I want a *future* with you—one I thought I could never want. But… I know how much you want kids right now, and why you need to do it now, and I can't… I can't promise to be good at any of this. I might need some time to adjust, but you don't *have* time and—'

She reached up to take his face in her hands and stopped him talking with a kiss.

'I'll freeze my eggs. Or we'll look into adoption when we're ready. We have options,' she said. 'What I want most of all is a loving, supportive relationship and a family—however that comes to pass. And I know you can be all that for me. I can wait while we figure out what that looks like. If that's what you want, too.'

'It is.' His words were fervent and his kiss possessive. 'God, Millie, it's what I want more than I've ever wanted anything.'

'Me too,' she admitted in a whisper. 'I never imagined…back when you were Charlie's annoying schoolfriend…that we could end up here. But I'm so glad we did.'

Giles smiled, and kissed her lightly again. 'Looks like the best man won, after all.'

She groaned at the joke, then wrapped an arm around his waist to lead him back up the aisle and out of the chapel into the frosty morning.

'Come on,' she said. 'Tabby and Mum will be going wild with curiosity up at the house. And I want to check in on Charlie, help him figure out what *he's* going to do now.'

'I think Charlie will be fine,' Giles said. 'But whatever he does next, I guarantee he won't be as happy as me. No man on earth could be right now.'

'And you thought you couldn't be a husband,' Millie said fondly. 'Keep talking like that and you'll do just fine.'

Giles laughed, and with their arms wrapped around each other they headed up to Howard Hall to find their best friend and start their new life. Together.

* * * * *

*Look out for the next story in the
Blame It on the Mistletoe duet*

Miss Right All Along
by Jessica Gilmore

*And if you enjoyed this story,
check out these other great reads from
Sophie Pembroke*

Socialite's Nine-Month Secret
Cinderella in the Spotlight
Best Man with Benefits

All available now!